Mighta Bin Wuss

Tales of the Boy Jimma

by Tony Clarke

NOSTALGIA Publications

TOFTWOOD • DEREHAM • NORFOLK

Published by:
NOSTALGIA PUBLICATIONS
(Terry Davy)
7 Elm Park, Toftwood,
Dereham, Norfolk
NR19 1NB

First impression: October 1998

ISBN 0 947630 21 X

Design and typesetting:
NOSTALGIA PUBLICATIONS

Printed by:
PAGE BROS. (NORWICH) LTD.
Mile Cross Lane,
Norwich,
Norfolk NR6 6SA

Dedicated to my wife Pat

Contents

Acknowledgements

It could be said that the person who really started this project was my great uncle Alf from whom, via my father, I inherited a countryman's smock.

This wonderful old garment, with its intricate needlework around collar, shoulders and cuffs, could have qualified for display in any museum of rural life.

However, it came into my possession at a time during my youth when that great smock-clad humorist Sidney Grapes was in his prime and my personal ambition was to become either a clergyman or a comedian.

Cracking jokes whilst wearing a garment resembling a surplice seemed the ideal compromise while I earned a living as a journalist with the Eastern Daily Press!

For more than 40 years I have related these stories at village variety shows, WI meetings and similar gatherings, adding to my store of anecdotes with the help of those many good East Anglians whose conversations have begun: "Have you heard the one about…?" or "My father used to tell the story of…"

The humble and accident-prone character of the Boy Jimma has evolved over a long period. He has achieved some notoriety in recent years with my membership of The Press Gang, that traditional troupe of troubadours who, led by Keith Skipper, peddle their squit around the region's village halls.

I make no pretence that this book is in any way historically authentic. It is simply a tribute to those many kind people who, over the years, have demonstrated to me that the East Anglian's sense of humour is, possibly uniquely, a triumph for the gentle art of laughing at yourself.

It seemed right that Jimma's exploits should be handed down for posterity in print, and I have many people to thank for their help in the production of this book.

There is, for example, Terry Davy, of Nostalgia Publications, who kindly agreed to publish this offering .

Then there is Jean Turner, of Toft Monks, whose book A Trip Down the Garden Path provided an illuminating insight into that social phenomenon, the privy.

Then there are her neighbours, Andrew and Jill Giller, who permitted us to use their disused privy for some "location shots".

The excellent Beccles and District Museum provided the school desk and location for Young Jimma's schooling, while All Saints Church, Worlingham, was the ideal setting for his first date with the Gal 'Liza.

Robert Tilney, of that long established Beccles gunsmith's business, R Tilney & Son, supplied a thankfully de-activated 12-bore shotgun as a much appreciated "prop" for Jimma's sinister advance upstairs with murderous intent.

And a co-operative and docile cow called Blanche posed helpfully - by kind permission of her "agent", herdsman John Wharton, of that wonderful farm dairy, R.H. and J Cundy, of Ditchingham - while being photographed from every conceivable angle.

But *Mighta Bin Wuss* is nothing if not a family enterprise involving the Clarke and Robins clan.

The pictures are the extremely professional work of Peter Robins. Some of his "models" posed posthumously in the snapshots he copied from my family album, and I sincerely hope are in no way demeaned by the use I have made of them.

Baby Jimma is my father, a group of Clarkes pose around a Ransome's traction engine in the family woodyard at Swaffham in the 1920s, my maternal grandfather, photographed at Hardingham, presents the image I had in mind for the kindly Farmer Greengrass and five stalwarts from Attleborough Civil Defence pose proudly.

Two ladies of whom I have very fond memories, my maternal grandmother and Aunt Rose, raise their sombre skirts for an extremely decorous paddle in the sea.

For Peter's contemporary creative work he had to look no further for his models than his son and my grandson, Edward, my daughter Tina, my elder son Jeremy and my wife Pat. Daughter-in-law Jill helped with "make-up" and moral support.

All of them posed with great enthusiasm, displaying a heart-warming sense of fun - along with a disturbing family talent for looking "sorft"!

My children, including younger son Tim, who wisely declined the opportunity of "stardom" in this book, have grown up with the Jimma stories. But my greatest debt of gratitude is owed to my wife Pat, to whom I dedicate this book.

Her fortitude and patience in tolerating Jimma throughout all these years, and her active encouragement in the production of this irreverent work have soared well above and beyond the call of duty.

Tony Clarke

A picture of youthful piety greeted the Vicar as he entered Young Jimma's bedroom. But was the boy really at prayer? "Sorry, we're oonly got one pot, Vicar!"

5

Foreword *by Keith Skipper*

Cider with Rosie put on record the England that was traded for the petrol engine. A half of mild with Jimma reminds us how the East Anglian countryside has been drained of much of its colour in too short a time.

Jimma may well be flattered or embarrassed by such grandiose literary comparisons, but I know enough about Laurie Lee and his Cotswolds upbringing to make them.

This is no cosy roses-round-the-door pastoral eulogy penned by a rustic remnant leaning on the broken gatepost of times past. It is a stirring tribute to a fast vanishing world which fashioned virtues out of austerity and found humour in adversity. Truly squit, wit - and plenty more.

Happily, Jimma is still with us to preach the proper gospel, in an epic opus such as this or on public platforms where his "warts-and-all" presentations transcend the usual mix of village hall drollery and country pub banter.

I came late to the prodigious verbal talents of Jimma as he stepped into the regular spotlight with my Press Gang concert party of local entertainers. The mantle of rural sage sits easily on him despite all the self-denigration running through many of his reflections.

He is justifiably proud of family roots steeped in country ways, many of them emanating from his family motto: "That sometimes pay yew to look sorfter than yew really are".

Infinitely preferable to that grubby urban trend of always pretending to be something you most definitely are not.

In these pages trimmed with deep and durable affection - Jimma has no truck with the passing fancy - our bucolic buccaneer admits to countless shortcomings when judged by orthodox standards.

He was a sickly child, constantly reminded that he ought to be neither seen nor heard. He took such advice too literally during village school days notable more for Jimma's failure to turn up than for any prowess in a classroom ruled over by the fearsome Ernest Swishem.

Efforts to find work were dogged by misadventure. The same pattern emerged in his pursuit of true love in the homely shape of the Gal 'Liza. Other escapades betrayed an innocence and shyness destined to complicate the most straightforward of matters.

But if Jimma was clumsy in word and deed, a simple trust in human nature coupled with an innate sense of goodness had to bring just rewards.

This vibrant volume is a celebration of Jimma's emergence as a respected pillar of his community. Chuckles of admiration have replaced the laughter of derision.

They listen now to learn from a true survivor of an age when everything went slower just in case you weren't quick enough to take it all in at one go.

Jimma enlightens and entertains. At his own pace and on his own terms. Now that's what I call getting on in a funny old world!

Keith Skipper, Cromer, 1998

1. Jimma's World

In Jimma's world it was possible for the occupant of the privy, a functional little shack at the bottom of the garden, to absorb much information from the little squares of newspaper which hung from a nail in the wall. Unfortunately, the end of the story was often missing

We dun't travel far but we're sin plenty o' life. Variations of this remark have been heard many thousands of times on the lips of home loving East Anglians.

The Boy Jimma was one of them. His world was largely centred on his home village, from which he ventured only rarely.

But in the course of a long and full life, rich in experience if not in money, the fates often seemed to be involved in a conspiracy to ensure that his existence would never become boring or predictable.

Village life was self-sufficient, primitive, ruled by the seasons, full of hard work and down to earth humour. An almost suffocatingly close knit community - but never predictable!

The name Jimma had been handed down through generations of the male line of our hero's family. Like his ancestors before him he spent his early life being known as Young Jimma - or simply "the boy".

This book is the story of his hazardous progress through half a lifetime's "apprenticeship" before he inherited from his father the name "Ow Jimma" which would mark him out as the head of the family.

With that title went the distinction of being generally regarded as the "village idiot", a dubious honour which had also been handed down through the generations of Jimma's family.

On those many occasions in his declining years when Jimma would regale his family, or anybody else who would listen, with stories from his youth, he would invest his reminiscences with the rose coloured tint of nostalgia, amplifying his successes and glossing over his failures. "That sometimes pay yer to look sorfter than yew really are," he would confide.

But we leap ahead of ourselves in our eagerness to explore the character of our hero. This modest volume is not concerned with his later life but with his early years. And the intention is to "tell it as it really was", and not as Jimma liked to remember it.

He was born, as he liked to tell people, at a "very arly earge." The remark was not so ridiculous as it might have sounded.

In old East Anglia babies were often born with a slightly "knowing" look. They came equipped with a kind of inherited native cunning.

This was not so much a measurable intelligence as a kind of inbred knowledge of the countryside and country ways. It developed in the womb and showed itself later in life as a tendency towards homespun common sense philosophy and a warped, introverted and sometimes unintentional sense of humour.

Instinct, you see. They knew, without being told, what life in the countryside was going to be like. Hard work, not many luxuries, but a few good laughs along the way.

In short, East Anglian babies either "knew a thing or two" about the world at birth, or they had a natural ability to pick up the mood of resignation in a mother whose muscular arms and work-worn hands may have been cradling her eighth or ninth infant.

Another mouth to feed, and where was that lazy good-for-nothing husband? Down the pub, you might know. And him only having done a 12-hour working day staring at the plump bottoms of two Suffolk Punches drawing a plough backwards and forwards across the 10-acre field. Idle bugger! And all for about three bob a week (15 pence).

Anyway, from Father's vantage point they (the Suffolk Punches) probably reminded him of the landlady at the Pig and Whistle. When she walked her bum, swathed in a comfortable skirt, looked like two piglets trying to get out of a sack.

Well, there wasn't time to fret about him. Mother would have to feed the baby then get out and help milk the cows. The villagers would be beating a path to the farmhouse kitchen door early next morning with their little enamel cans to collect the milk.

And the farm butter, all nice and fatty and full of taste. Nobody had heard of that strange dried up girl so popular nowadays, Polly Unsaturated.

East Anglian babies were born into families which, for generations, had travelled no more than a few miles from their own largely self-sufficient communities. The village, possessing farms, school, shop, pub, church and village "hut", provided for all their simple needs in employment, education, food, drink, social and spiritual refreshment - but not necessarily in that order.

They were born into a world where the sanitary arrangements were primitive, to say the least. In fact, it is a wonder they survived to see a ripe old age - as many of them did - considering all the health scares which have crept into the human food chain in the paranoid 1980s and 1990s.

At a time when food comes ready wrapped, supermarkets are as hygiene-conscious as hospitals, and shop assistants are obliged to use gloves and tongs to dispense such comestables as cannot be shrink wrapped, we worry ourselves silly about foot and mouth, scrapy, BSE, salmonella and whatever else the scientists can think up.

And well we might, considering that those same scientists had previously advised our farmers that it was perfectly safe to feed all manner of unnatural foods to our cattle and spread various unlikely chemicals on our land.

It wasn't like that in Jimma's day. Life may have been filthy, but at least it was honest, natural, organic filth!

There was no electricity, mains water or sewerage. In the cottage light was provided by lamps and the family, up at dawn, was usually in bed early.

Mother, in her whitewashed cottage kitchen, concocted good wholesome meals with the most rudimentary equipment, a blackened oven, perhaps, under which two smokey paraffin stoves provided the heat. Or a black leaded range in which the fire, glinting angrily from between the bars of a tiny grate, would heat the oven.

In the corner of the scullery was the copper in which she boiled the clothes - or the beetroot, or the potatoes - and nearby was the mangle with which she wrung the washing dry.

She knew exactly what kind of fertiliser had been spread on the garden from which she took her vegetables. Some of it came from the very same Suffolk Punches which Father followed at ploughing time, and some of it - Heaven preserve us! - from the family's own privy.

Alongside her cottage garden ran a smelly ditch, which became stagnant or dried up altogether in summertime. A water butt, its contents covered with a film of green slime, collected rainwater from the "troffins". A small stream ran across the bottom of the garden.

From a nail on an outhouse wall hung the tin bath in which the family conducted its weekly head-to-toe ablutions. Bath night, either in front of the kitchen fire or in the draughty scullery, could be a colourful occasion.

The occupant of the bath would be reddened from the waist down by the scalding water which Mother ladled from the copper, and blue with cold from the waist up because of the gale which blew under the scullery door.

There is little wonder that Jimma's father didn't take a bath any more often than he could help. So rare were his ceremonial immersions in the tub that they could easily be confused, by his way of speaking, with his annual "bathday" by which he grew a year older.

The privy was at the bottom of the garden, sited as far away from the house as possible. It was a small, picturesque but malodorous structure covered by a rambler rose in a desperate attempt to mask the all pervading aroma which arose from the bucket discreetly hidden under the wooden seat inside.

Access to this humble house of relief was via a door attached by a simple latch. There being no lock or bolt, it was generally considered advisable to sing or whistle whilst inside. This would let others know that you were comfortably - and privately, you hoped - ensconsed on a seat which had been worn smooth by generations of large country bottoms.

Questioned about the absence of a lock on his privy door Jimma's father was known to respond: "Why should we hev one? We hen't hed nuthin pinched outa there yit!"

Expeditions to the privy in the middle of the night were major adventures, especially if the weather was bad and your hurricane lamp blew out. No wonder there was a marble topped wash stand, complete with flowery china jug and bowl, in every bedroom and a chamber pot of similar design, otherwise known as a "guzunder" or jerry, beneath every bed. They came as a matching set.

Once inside the privy there was little incentive to stay long although there was a risk of suffering literary as well as physical constipation. Impaled on a nail would be a sheaf of neatly cut squares of newspaper.

The more literate privy occupant, his attention attracted by half a headline or story on one sheet, might engage in a fruitless search through the toilet paper for the other half - only to conclude that it had already been used. You could freeze to death with curiosity wondering how a tantalisingly interesting story ended.

Such was the cottage home into which Jimma was born. From his bedroom window, snugly under the eaves, he could see across the lane and into the cluttered smithy, its whitewashed walls hidden behind a mass of tools, horseshoes, collars, harnesses, brasses and wagon wheels.

He was woken each morning by the sound of the blacksmith at work at his forge; the roar of the bellows, the clang of hammer on anvil, the hiss of steam as the iron "tyre" of a wagon wheel was cooled and shrunk into place. As a boy he spent hours watching the blacksmith, hoping for some small job to come his way.

Truth to tell, Jimma was not your average "knowing" countryside infant. He was a loner, innocent of the natural instincts which came in most babies born into a farming family, and full of wide-eyed wonder at the world around him. For this reason he was well qualified to become the village idiot.

Today, every East Anglian community should have its ceremonial smock-clad village idiot to become part of the village scenery and to entertain with homespun wit and wisdom in the Pig and Whistle. It would be a wonderful attraction for tourists.

In Jimma's family the tradition was genuine and greatly prized. His great grandfather had been Ow Jimma when his grandfather was Young Jimma. Then Grandfather had become Ow Jimma and Father was Young Jimma. Now Father was Ow Jimma and here was his young 'un.

Young Jimma, the subject of our story, was eventually to get married, grow "owd" and have a son of his own. Being a great man for family tradition, he named him Fred!

But, for now, let's get back to his beginnings. At birth he was small, wizened and weedy. Father took one look at him and observed: "If I'd 'a bin a fisherman I'd 'a chucked this one back!" But he wasn't, and he didn't, so Jimma survived to enjoy the life now to be related.

2. He Mearke Yer Sick

Propped up in front of the camera, the Baby Jimma did not look too comfortable. But then, he was not accustomed to being swathed in such a pile of posh but borrowed clothes

Jimma was a sickly child, as many were in his day. But our hero was sickly in more ways than one; sick of body and wayward of mind.

"He mearke everybody sick, he do," his father was heard to observe, with notable lack of sympathy.

They were a poor family, but proud. So poor that they could not afford respectable clothes for a growing infant. So proud that, inadequately attired as he invariably was, Jimma was never allowed out in public.

Indeed, he was four years old before the family could afford to buy him a hat which covered his head decently enough for him to be seen looking out of the window.

On one occasion as a baby - and only one - was he decked out in the finest clothes which his family had borrowed so that he would have his photograph taken with "one o' them new fangled camera things."

The problem was that the only people who could be persuaded to lend Jimma's parents the necessary baby clothes for the photograph were an elderly couple who had been very proud of their baby daughter.

She had grown up into a "slummeken grit mawther" but they had kept her baby clothes as a reminder of what a bonny baby she had been.

"That dornt matters whether the garmints were mearde fer a boy or a gal," said Jimma's mother. "They look noice an' at his earge he won't know the diff'rence.

"Anyhow," she added as an afterthought: "I wus really hooping fer a pritty little mawther and blast if that din't tarn out ter be Jimma."

It was, after all, an age of great propriety when children were expected to be seen and not heard - or, in Jimma's case, preferably neither seen nor heard.

Women, whatever their station in life, were clothed from neck to ankles, and usually wore hats as well. It was only with great reluctance that Jimma's father was persuaded that it was fit and proper for his wife to roll up her sleeves far enough to bury her arms in the washing tub.

So little sunshine had warmed Jimma's back and so little fresh air had filled his lungs that when the time came for him to start at the village school he was a pale and unprepossessing specimen of the human race.

He was a puny infant with a scraggy physique, raggedy clothes and a seemingly permanent candlestick descending from his nose across which, having usually forgotten his handkerchief, he would, from time to time, draw his inadequate sleeve.

He was, in short, a very unsavoury child indeed, and although his teacher, Mr Ernest Swishem, was a punctillious and strict disciplinarian, there is little doubt that he considered Jimma's high rate of absenteeism to be his most endearing feature.

"He's less use than the space he takes up," the harrassed teacher confided to his wife, the school secretary.

In fact, Jimma was away from school so often that his mother wrote an all-purpose excuse note which she used on every occasion.

It began: "Dear Mr Swishem Sir," (for she was a very respectful woman), and continued: "My Jimma can't come because he hen't bin. When we're giv 'im suffin to mearke 'im go, an' that 'a took effect, he'll come."

Consistent she might have been with her excuse notes, truthful she decidedly was not. Delicate though his health was, Jimma's absences were as often caused by his father's desire for a bit of help around the farmyard as they were by acute constipation.

And even Jimma, an ungifted student and reluctant worker, often found the prospect of "mucking out" the pigs preferable to wrestling with his times tables under the jaundiced eye of Mr Swishem.

After all, reasoned his father, he would probably end up working on a farm after he left school so he might as well get in a bit of free work experience even if he was only five years old. He was, in fact, doing his son a favour, the way he saw it.

Largely because of his sheltered early upbringing, Jimma was an innocent abroad - even in the claustrophobic community of the village and village school. A community where everybody knew everybody else and most inhabitants were related to each other (either within Holy Matrimony or as a result of adventures the wrong side of the blanket).

A community so rife with gossip and watchful for real or imagined improprieties that a man could ruin a woman's reputation simply by inadvertently leaving his bike propped up against her garden fence.

The fact that Jimma remained largely aloof from all this parochial intrigue throughout his long life was due partly to his own innocent nature and partly to his lifelong discomfort with some of the more basic functions of human existence, especially sex.

Despite the fact that it was going on around him all the time in the farmyard, it was not easy for his infant mind to comprehend why a bull should want to start clambering about on a cow, or why a sow should look so pleased with herself after a visit to the boar. And the thought of linking these phenomena to the sudden appearance of calves and piglets a few months later was quite beyond him.

It was only when a sudden population explosion occurred in the hutches where he was allowed to keep rabbits that it began to dawn on him that the arrival of the "little 'uns" had something to do with the presence of both male and female adults in the same hutch. But since he couldn't tell the one from the other there was very little he could do about the problem.

His parents adopted a tight lipped attitude to the subject. To be fair to them, they had at least resolved not to fill their innocent son's head with fantasies about storks or gooseberry bushes, but rather to answer his questions truthfully as and when they came. They just didn't come, mainly because Jimma was too embarrassed to ask them. The subject was simply not on the family's agenda.

One day, on his return from school, Jimma innocently inquired: "Ma, where do I come from?" His mother's ruddy complexion reddened. This was the moment she had been dreading, but to her credit, she resolved to give him all the intimate details as she knew them, and as they applied to birds, bees, domestic animals - and humans.

Turning away from the stove in which a beef pudding was cooking, she sat down, drew her son to her, and rambled on for half an-hour or more, picking her words carefully, warming to her subject and exploring every human implication which occurred to her. It was by far the longest conversation she had ever had with Jimma, or was ever likely to have with him.

It ended unexpectedly when she finally inquired why it had suddenly occurred to Jimma to ask his big question on that particular day. "Why?" responded her totally bewildered son. "Well, we hed a new boy at school terday an' he come from Barsham, so I jist wondered where I come from!"

Jimma's knowledge of sex was, at best, rudimentary following his mother's tortuous explanation. Subsequently the subject somehow became confused with religion, a matter on which he had much greater opportunity to be well informed since the family went to church every Sunday to be threatened with hellfire from the pulpit by the vicar and rural dean, the formidable Canon Horatio Gunn.

In addition, Jimma was a reluctant pupil of the Sunday school where he came under the benign and undemanding influence of the devout Miss Winifred Bell whose brother Charlie, the sexton and gravedigger, rejoiced in the nickname of "Dinga".

This came partly from his surname and partly from his habit of threatening any miscreant he caught up to mischief in the churchyard with a "dinga the lug".

Jimma was such a poor pupil in Sunday school that Miss Bell could remember only one occasion when he actually took the initiative and asked a question.

"Yew know them songs we sing in church," he remarked one day in class. "Why der we allus sing 'Our Men' at the end of 'em? Why dun't we sometimes sing 'Our Wimmen'?"

It was a question which Miss Bell had never been called upon to consider before. "I spose thass because there're called hymns," she improvised. "If they wus called Hars I reckon we'd sing 'Our Wimmen'."

This piece of rudimentary theology seemed to satisfy Jimma. But on another occasion he really came unstuck - and it was his poor memory, along with the confusion between sex and religion, which got him into trouble.

Returning home one Sunday afternoon Jimma told his mother that, during Sunday school, Miss Bell had asked him a testing question. "Jimma," she had said: "Who made you?"

"What did you say?" inquired Mother.

"Well, arter orl them things you told me about the bads an' the bees and the animals bein' like human beins, I said I s'posed my father did," replied the boy.

"Blast boy yew shun't 'a said thet," admonished his shocked Mother. "Next time she arst yew who mearde yer, yew tell her God did; thass what she want to hear!"

The following week, on his return from Sunday school, Jimma reported: "She arst me that question agin."

"What'd yew tell 'er this time?" asked Mother again, with some trepidation.

Jimma's eyes twinkled with the thought that he may have got something almost right. "I said I couldn't rightly remember but I knew damn well that wun't me father!"

One thing that could be said in favour of Canon Gunn was that he was good at making house calls. Once a week, around tea time, the best china would be brought out and the Vicar would be entertained by Mother to tea and biscuits in the parlour when solicitous inquiries would be made as to the physical and spiritual health of the entire family.

Jimma would invariably be sent to bed early on these occasions and, unable to sleep, would listen to the low hum of voices from downstairs.

One day Canon Gunn inquired specifically after Jimma's health, a sniffly cold having kept the boy away from church the previous Sunday.

"Tellin' the trewth vicar, he in't too keen on charch when he in't feelin' tew sharp," said Mother. "Thet tend to be a bit parky in there. He's gone to bed but yew can go up an' hev a talk ter 'im if yer want."

With difficulty the vicar, whose appreciation of good food was renowned, negotiated his portly frame up the narrow staircase which led directly from the parlour to Jimma's tiny bedroom.

He was immediately struck by the scene which confronted him. There, beside the empty bed knelt Jimma, his head in his hands. The vicar, much moved by this display of private piety, sank to his knees on the other side of the bed and bowed his head.

Whereupon Jimma looked up, startled. "What are yew a'doin' on, vicar?" he inquired. "The same as you are, my son," responded Canon Gunn in hushed tones. "Blast I hope you en't," exclaimed the lad; "We're only got one pot!"

Jimma was later to wonder why the vicar never again honoured him with a private visit, even after he had missed church.

In one respect, and one only, Jimma did show a degree of youthful ambition and energy. His father, a regular patron of the local saleyard where he usually bought and sold with disastrous consequences to his already sparse resources, had acquired a redundant beach hut which had served as a changing room for Edwardian bathing belles.

It had been trundled down the beach at Southwold and into the shallows to preserve the modesty of its occupants when, clad in their voluminous bathing costumes, they took a dip in the sea for their health's sake.

Father had converted this conveyance into the family privy and had stationed it at the bottom of the garden on the bank of the stream, omitting to remove the wheels. Jimma's one youthful ambition was to push the privy in the stream.

One day, when the place seemed deserted, he took his opportunity, tiptoeing down the garden path, applying his shoulder to the privy and giving one huge shove. He did not wait to see the structure roll ponderously down the bank and into the water.

For some hours Jimma was nowhere to be seen. On his furtive return he was summoned to stand before his father who went straight to the point. "Who pushed the privy in the river?" he inquired, stern of countenance. "I don't know," responded Jimma, trying unsuccessfully to look innocent.

"Boy," said Father, keeping his temper firmly under control and determined to display the benefits of his own half-remembered education at the village school: "I'm gorn ter tell yew a story. A lot of years ago, in America, there was a boy called George Washington an' he chopped down his father's favourite cherry tree."

"Now when his father arst him who dunnit, he say: 'Father, I cannot tell a lie, I dunnit. I chopped yar cherry tree down.' An' his father din't punish 'im because he told the trewth."

"Now boy," continued Owd Jimma to Young Jimma. "I'll arst yer agin; who pushed the privy in the river? An' just yew remember George Washington."

"Well, seein' as 'ow yew put it like that, I did," admitted the boy. "I pushed the privy in the river." Whereupon his father immediately aimed a wild swing at Jimma's head, catching him a sharp blow round the lug.

Shocked by this unexpectedly violent reaction, Young Jimma burst into tears. "Why'd yer do that when George Washington didn't git punished?" he sobbed.

"Cos there's one big diff'rence 'twin yew an' George Washington," shouted Ow Jimma, with feeling. "His father wun't up the cherry tree at the time!"

As a result of this incident, however, Ow Jimma concluded that turning a beach hut into a privy had been a mistake. He therefore decided to "go modern" and get his friend Albert, the local builder, to put up a more substantial brick-built establishment at the bottom of his garden.

3. No Work at the Big House

Young Jimma had not been a gifted student at the village school. "The lamps may be lit but there in't nobodda at hoom!" concluded his father as the boy began his search for work.

At the age of 14 the time had come for Jimma to leave the village school and seek work. His school career had been undistinguished, his attendance irregular, and it would be accurate to report that neither he nor Mr Swishem were sad at this parting of their ways.

It would also be true to say that neither Jimma nor his father were particularly enamoured of the idea of working together on the family farm. Father was an impatient man and Jimma was none too sharp when it came to comprehending his instructions.

"That boy's as thick as they come," said Father, experiencing no great difficulty in hiding any trace of paternal pride. "If intelligence added up to a week I reckon he'd be about up to Tewsday night. He's half loight if yew arst me. The lamps may be lit in the winders but there in't noboby at hoom, if yew know what I mean."

But Jimma was not entirely friendless. He had much in common with a youth called "Jarge" who had also managed to go through school without absorbing any of the basic academic skills with which Mr Swishem had so laboriously attempted to equip his ill starred pupils.

Despite all the schoolmaster's best efforts Jarge had left school with virtually no "book larnin" at all. He also laboured under the additional handicap of being painfully shy.

But one attribute which he did possess in good measure was "a fair ow hid for figures". And later in life, once he had overcome his shyness, he was to become a successful and wealthy farmer with several thousand acres in his ownership and the proud boast that: "I can't read an' I can't write - but I can reckon!"

Jarge's later success in life could in no way be attributed to Jimma's influence. In fact, as we shall discover, their friendship almost led to Jarge having no life at all.

But, for the moment, Jimma and Jarge found themselves thrown into each other's company and, seeking employment together, they ventured nervously up the long drive which led to the "big house", a 16th century mansion which was the ancestral seat from which Lord and Lady Wymond-Hayme ran their large estate.

Perhaps, reasoned the two ill-equipped candidates, they might be able to get jobs as under gardeners, or something, then work their way up.

Nervously they mounted the steps to the hall's main entrance and pulled the huge wrought iron bell pull. A sound which resembled the striking of a dozen church clocks rang through the house.

With difficulty the two frightened boys resisted the temptation to rush straight home.

A tall, stiff and imposing butler, wearing a formal suit which looked as if it had been ironed on to him, answered their summons and glared down at them disdainfully. "Go round to the kitchen door," he commanded before Jimma or Jarge could get a word out. "We don't allow your sort at the front of the house."

So far so good. At least they hadn't been run off the premises by a pack of hunting dogs. And even better was to come. The kitchen door was opened to them by the gal 'Liza, a buxom wench who worked at the hall as a housemaid and in whom Jimma had shown more than a passing interest at school.

She smiled, just as if she recognised him, which Jimma doubted.

"Yew'd better come in then," said 'Liza. "But mind yew tearke yar bewts orf fust. We don't want yew a-dattyin' the floor."

With their boots and caps in their hands, they found themselves in a large kitchen. Gleaming cooking utensils hung above the shiny black leaded range in which a roaring fire peeped redly through the bars.

A wooden butter churn stood in one corner and at the enormous scrubbed wooden table, which dominated the centre of the room, stood the cook, a moon faced mean spirited woman of ample proportions indicative of a taste for sampling the products of her own oven.

Her face wore an expression sour enough to curdle the custard. Her practised hands and muscular arms were, at that moment, employed in kneading the dough for a beef dumplin. To Jimma it was a frightening sight. If those hands could do that to a mere lump of dough what couldn't they do to a man's dumplins, he wondered.

The butler strode into the room. Mistaking Jimma and Jarge for a couple of gipsies selling pegs or lucky charms, he said sternly: "Whatever it is you're selling, we don't want any of it. You'd better go away."

Jarge stood twisting his cap in his hands nervously, but Jimma plucked up courage. "We're come ter arst fer a job on the estearte," he said simply.

"Huh," exclaimed the butler unpromisingly. "You don't look very respectable to me, but then it isn't up to me to decide whether or not to employ you.

17

"The decision, of course, is His Lordship's, and he happens to be out at the moment, as is his agent." Then, realising that the two were just simple village lads, he added in a kindlier voice: "But I will ask Her Ladyship if she might consider you for some modest employment in the kitchen garden."

The butler disappeared and there followed an uncomfortable wait for his return. Nothing was said although 'Liza, seated in a corner and quietly sewing, kept looking at Jimma and giggling to herself. The cook bent to put her puddin' in the oven, displaying, as she did so, a rump similar in size to those which Jimma had seen between the shafts of a farm wagon.

The butler returned. "Her Ladyship will see you in the drawing room," he said with an expression of mild surprise on his face.

The drawing room was vast and full of heavy highly polished antique furniture with deep rugs on a polished floor.

Jimma and Jarge both planted their sock-clad feet firmly on a rug. It promptly slid away from under them and they fell heavily on their backsides.

Their faces red with embarrassment and shame, they rose with difficulty, brushing themselves down with their caps, touching their forelocks respectfully and muttering abject apologies.

Jarge looked as if he wished the floor could open up and swallow him. He stood mutely awaiting his fate, looking at Jimma to take a lead in this awe inspiring situation.

Her Ladyship, a tall thin austere figure in a long dress with pinched waist and puffed sleeves, sat bolt upright in a chair by the huge fireplace.

A graceful hand fluttered delicately across her lips to disguise the smile which was twitching the corners of her mouth. These clumsy oafs were enough to make anybody smile but her regal dignity must not be allowed to slip.

"You may approach," she said as Jimma and Jarge stood awkwardly by the door. "There is no need to be nervous. I hear you are seeking employment."

"Yis Ma'am, er Yer Leardyship," replied Jimma respectfully. Her Ladyship looked them up and down. They seemed sound in wind and limb. Perhaps the head gardener could find work for them in some humble way, she thought.

But Her Ladyship was a stickler for doing things by the book. If people were to be taken on, even in the humblest of positions, then all the correct protocol had to be observed. "Do you have any references?" she asked. "Pardon?" replied Jimma, bewildered but still polite.

Anxious to explain herself clearly, Her Ladyship enlarged on her question. "What I mean is this. I need to take down your particulars and study your testimonials."

Minutes later Jimma and Jarge were running back down the drive with the butler in hot pursuit. Struggling to do up his trousers, which he had removed in the mistaken belief that Her Ladyship had been suggesting a medical examination, Jimma gasped: "Yer know what Jarge? I still think with a bit more eddicearshun we mighta unnerstood them big wards an' got the job!"

Neither Jimma nor Jarge ever plucked up the courage to go back to the Big House to retrieve their boots, although Jimma did get his back some years later, and somewhat unexpectedly.

4. Ed Bless Us On Our Way

Only once, Jimma's mother accompanied a Sunday school outing. But though she and Miss Winifred Bell lifted their skirts most decorously for a paddle, they still maintained the utmost respectibility of dress

For those East Anglians who were prepared to walk to the coast, or could afford the train fare, employment, if they could get it at all, was a straight choice between the land and the sea. Both represented lives of hard work and poverty entirely at the mercy of the elements.

Norfolk and Suffolk are maritime counties and some of the world's hardiest seafarers have sailed from East Anglian shores, whether in times of peace or war.

Neither Jimma nor Jarge could be counted among East Anglia's noblest sea venturers. Jimma could only recall one occasion when he had even seen the sea, and that was when Miss Winifred Bell, in a rash moment of bravery, had decided to take the Sunday school on a day trip to Lowestoft.

Jimma, even though he came from a devout church-going family, had not learned much about the Scriptures during his attendance at Sunday school. In fact, his mother could remember only a few occasions when, on returning from Winifred's class, her son had mentioned anything of what he had heard.

"I know what God's name is," he had announced one Sunday. "Oh ah," said Mother, intrigued. "What do yew call him?"

"Ed," replied Jimma. "How d'yer mearke thet out?" asked Mother, now perplexed. "Well," said Jimma: "Miss Bell told us how ter talk ter Him terday. She say, 'Our Father, what art in Heaven, Hallo, Ed be Thy nearme. Thass how I knew; I ent daft yer know!"

In those days steam trains criss-crossed East Anglia, reaching parts from which they have long since disappeared. Tall funnelled engines hauled elderly gas-lit coaches along country branch lines, stopping at tiny village halts where the station staff, proud of their reputation for cleanliness, spent many of the hours between trains polishing the brasses and tending the gardens alongside the line wherein they grew their flowers, fruit and vegetables for the house.

And from which, in the due seasons of the year, they might supplement their modest incomes by selling the surplus produce to passengers.

The Sunday school outing had involved an eventful train journey. Discipline had largely broken down as Winifred and her brother "Dinga" failed miserably to contain the exuberance of their excited charges.

Various items of clothing were lost through the train windows on the way there and most of the children had consumed their picnic dinners, carefully prepared by their mothers and wrapped in a cloth, long before they arrived at the beach.

Several children got themselves lost during the day, and the search for them meant that the party missed its train home and had to catch a later one.

Some of Winifred's charges, having forgotten their bathing costumes, had gone for a paddle and ventured too far into the sea with the result that they had to travel home in wet trousers or skirts. Others had suffered "little accidents" which had produced much the same result.

There was sand everywhere and many of the children subsequently caught sniffles. On one thing, and one only, there was complete agreement between Winifred, "Dinga" and the children's angry parents - there would never again be a Sunday school outing to the seaside.

Now Jimma and Jarge, still jobless, decided that if their future didn't seem to lie in the soil, it just might come from the sea. Ill equipped for later life in academic terms, they had picked up a smattering of knowledge about their region, not all of it accurate, from the pundits who gathered in the tap room at the Pig and Whistle.

Young Jimma and Jarge had been known to sneak in there, without their parents' knowledge. They would sit quietly in a corner and listen to the conversations of the worldly wise.

Their sneaky excursions into what Jimma's mother described as "a low den o' vice" ended abruptly when they slipped into the tap room one night only to find Jimma's father, the reigning Ow Jimma, holding centre stage among a circle of rustic friends. Ow Jimma was giving voice to one of his favourite subjects - women.

"Yew're gotta treat 'em hard," he advised decisively. "Discipline, thass what they unnerstand. Show 'em who's the marster in the house."

At which point Ow Jimma suddenly spotted his son trying to sneak furtively out of the room. "Whatta yew a-doin' on here boy?" he called. 'Yar Ma'll hev suffin ter say when she find out yew're bin in here."

Finding himself in a tight corner, even Jimma could think quickly on occasions. "She're sent me ter tell yew ter git hoom 'cos if yew dun't yar supper's a-gorn out fer the pigs," he said defiantly.

Ow Jimma did not want to lose face in front of his friends. But, weighing up his options, he concluded that the prospect of losing his supper to the pigs just about outweighed the embarrassment he would suffer if he left the pub at that moment.

"Well, I'd better be a-gorn hoom then," he muttered. As the door closed behind Ow Jimma, Young Jimma and Jarge the landlord turned to the assembled company and remarked quietly: "So let that be a lesson tew all on yer. Discipline, thass what wimmen need!"

The incident had its sequel when Ow Jimma and Young Jimma got home.

"Where hev yew tew bin?" asked Mother. "Well I'd only jist slipped inter the Pig an' Whistle when the boy cum in an' towed me if I din't git hoom yew'd be a-givin' my supper ter the pigs," explained Father. Mother angrily dished out two hefty clips round the lug; one to her husband for "hangin' about down that awful pub an' leadin' yar son inter bad ways," and the other to Young Jimma for telling lies.

"I never said yer father's supper was a-gorn out ter the pigs," she said. "Mind yew, thass a good idea seein' as how he spend orl his time in that den o' vice."

Young Jimma also got a clout from his father for getting him into trouble. "An' let that be a lesson tew yer," said Ow Jimma. "Discipline, thass what yew need!"

But Jimma and Jarge had already made enough surrepticious trips to the Pig and Whistle to have heard many wonderful stories of far away places.

They had heard that the North Sea was alive with herring, that the harbours of Yarmouth and Lowestoft were choked with drifters, and that there was a good living to be had from fishing.

What they hadn't heard was that a drifterman's life could be even harder than that of a farm labourer.

"I reckon I cd set around on a fishin' boot all day," remarked Jimma. "They en't verra big so there can't be a lot ter dew. Whadya say we try Loostaff?"

So next day the two intrepid landlubbers set out to walk to the coast. It was to prove an unexpectedly long, eventful and roundabout journey.

Came the evening of the first day and the two were getting tired. "Blast if my ow bewts ent pinchin'," said Jimma. "I reckon we'd better rest awhile."

Sitting by the side of the narrow dusty country road the two job seekers began to realise that the pangs of hunger were advancing fast and they had not thought to bring either money or their supper.

"An' blast if my ow stomach ent startin' ter think my thrut's bin cut," remarked Jimma. "Whatta we gorn ter dew fer wittals."

Standing up, he looked around at the deserted countryside. There wasn't a house in sight. But the field on the other side of the hedge contained row upon row of potatoes. "I reckon we cud mearke a fire an' cook a few spuds," he told Jarge. "Or if the wust come ter the wust we cd eat 'em raw. I'll creep through the hedge and dig a few up time yew keep an eye open in cearse sombodda come."

With that, Jimma stooped, wriggled his way through the hedge and disappeared.

He was gone, as East Anglians would say, "the best part of a tidy while", grovelling on all fours and scrabbling at the roots with his hands. Meantime, the exertions of the day were catching up on Jarge. His head nodded, his eyes closed. Minutes later they opened to behold the alarming sight of a portly village constable propping his bike against a tree and approaching with measured tread. A cry of warning died in Jarge's throat as the policeman greeted him.

"Whatta yew settin hare weartin for, Christmas?" he asked. "Yew look like somebodda whass up ter no good. I hoope yew ent thinkin about doin a bit of poochin 'cos dew yew are I'll hev suffin ter say about it."

Jarge, who was not a quick thinker at the best of times, could find no words to explain himself. Dumbstruck, he looked vacantly at the policeman then at the hole in the hedge. His eyes opened wide with horror as Jimma's scraggy backside appeared and began forcing its way through to be followed by a red face wearing an expression of triumph.

"I're got 'em," he announced before, having already incriminated himself, he spotted the policeman. "So I see," observed the officer conversationally. "Now I reckon that'd be in yar best interests to accompany me quietly ter the stearshun so's I can mearke out a charge sheet."

In those days every small East Anglian market town had its own courthouse, and the following day, having spent their first ever night in a cell, Jimma and Jarge both appeared before the bench.

"Theft is a most serious offence, however hungry you might have been," declared the squire, an imposing figure in tweed jacket and plus fours, who dispensed judgement with the aid of a few lesser mortals who were important enough to be magistrates but generally not brave enough to question his decisions.

"Since you are unlikely to be able to pay a fine I have no option but to send you to prison for seven days." The horrified pair were led away and taken to the town's bridewell, a small and ancient house of correction where simple sinners like Jimma and Jarge would pass their sentences and more serious criminals would be accommodated briefly before transfer to larger prisons.

There they were incarcerated in a cell which already had one occupant, a morose and scruffy individual. Several hours passed before anybody spoke.

Eventually the cell's older inhabitant broke the ice. "Whatta yew tew in for?" he asked gruffly. "Nickin a few spuds," replied Jimma. "How longa yew got?" inquired the man of few words, keeping up the interrogation. "A week," said Jimma.

This brief burst of conversation was followed by more hours of silence and it wasn't until next morning that Jimma thought the time had come to continue the exchange, curiosity having finally overcome his native reserve. "Whatta yew in clink for?" he asked the scruffy individual. "Rearpe," was the succinct reply.

"How longa yew got?" continued Jimma. "Six yare," came the answer. "Bugger me!" exploded Jimma without intending the implied invitation: "Whadya hev a whole field o' the stuff?"

The "rearpist" having decided that it was not in his best interests to advise the innocent Jimma that the kind of "rearpe" he was in for did not grow in fields, there was no further conversation before two burly policemen arrived to take him on his onward journey.

"He wus a rum bloke if yer arst me," was all Jimma could say as he and Jarge passed the remainder of their sentence in peace, angered only by this enforced interruption to their own journey towards the coast.

"A real rum bloke - an' anyway, he talked tew much!"

5. For Those in Peril....

In his later years, when recalling his exploits on a herring drifter, the Boy Jimma was inclined to "gild the lily", investing his own role in an undistinguished voyage with a heroism he did not deserve.

The sight which greeted Jimma and Jarge when they eventually arrived at Lowestoft without further mishap, offered the greatest possible contrast to the quiet country village they had left.

The fish market was a hive of activity as East Anglia's silver harvest was brought in. Great barrels of fish were everywhere. The outer harbour was crammed with ships, their masts, rigging and grimy funnels resembling nothing more than a gently swaying forest.

You could have walked across the water on their decks, if you'd a mind to - and if you could have done so without being challenged. Derricks swung the baskets of fish ashore as each ship competed for the honour of bringing home the most herring that day.

The ships' catches, and the prices paid for the fish, would all be faithfully recorded in the local paper.

Merchants were bidding briskly. Everywhere the market was a soggy and chaotic scene full of water, ice, fish and people.

Away by the sea shore the Scots fishergirls, down from Aberdeen for the harvest, worked at long tables gutting the fish. Tough weatherbeaten women with huge aprons and muscular arms, they had amazingly nimble fingers and vocabularies which would have shocked the most outspoken regulars at the Pig and Whistle.

It was the heyday of the herring. Although they didn't know it, Jimma and Jarge were witnessing a historic spectacle of which their children and grandchildren would know nothing.

They saw it all with wonderment. Could they really become part of all this? Well, they had got here so at least they had to give it a try.

But did any skipper want a couple of extra hands? Especially hands with no experience of a seagoing life, having been more accustomed to trying to avoid work on the land. "They in't a-gorn ter want us, are they bor?" remarked Jarge, his natural shyness getting the better of him.

They stood on the quay and wondered what to do, two lost souls engulfed in a whirlpool of activity.

Nobody wanted to know these strange figures up from the country, or had time to talk to them. They were in the way.

Then Jimma saw, down in a corner of the harbour, as if hiding from its bigger and better sisters, one of the smallest, oldest and rustiest of all these valiant little coal driven steamers.

It seemed somehow forgotten. Indeed, it did not look as if it had put to sea for some time. Yet Jimma could see, framed in the wheelhouse window, the figure of a grizzled old seaman. Cap on head, pipe in mouth, he looked like the mould in which the face and figure of Popeye might have been cast.

Then Jimma's wandering eye lit on something else. The name on the vessel's stern was - The Gal 'Liza! Could this be a good omen?

Jimma and Jarge approached this humble vessel tentatively. "Dew yew stay on the bank time I gorn arst if he want a coupla extra men," Jimma instructed Jarge. "Yew bein so shy by nearture."

Jimma climbed awkwardly down on to the deck and knocked politely on the wheelhouse door. He had always been brought up to know his manners, especially when he wanted something. And he did want something right now; a job.

A weatherworn wrinkled face fringed with grey whiskers suddenly appeared through a nearby hatch. "Git yew orfa this hare vessel at once!" it shouted. At the same moment the captain opened the wheelhouse door and yelled: "Howd yar row Billy. Yew know duzzy well thass bad luck ter be rude to visitors even if they dun't look as though they're ever bin on a ship afore."

Then, to Jimma: "Dun't yew tearke no notice a Billy. He'd be a good engineer if he din't git sozzled an want to start a fight evera time he go ashore. He allus think when strearngers come aboard they must be people what we owe money tew.'

Then, suddenly a little less sure of himself, he added: "Yew ent, are yer? Somebody what we owe money tew, I mean."

"No," said Jimma, failing to spot these clear indications that 'The Gal 'Liza' might not be a happy choice of ship. "What I're come about is a job. I want ter join yar crew."

The old man of the sea looked surprised. It was not often that an apparently able bodied man offered himself for service on board the Gal 'Liza without being more or less press ganged. "The boy must be tew fish short o' a cran," he thought, perceptively.

Then, eyeing this fresh faced country lad up and down, he remarked unpromisingly: "I hatta say yew dun't look a mucher.

"I dun't spose yew know one end of a ship from th'other. Still, beggars carn't be chusers an' we hent hed a lotta luck leartely. P'raps if I took yer on our luck might chearnge."

"Mind yew," he continued, trying hard to be fair: "I're gotta warn yer that'd mean working longa ow Billy an' he's more often drunk than sober."

Then Jimma remembered Jarge, still standing self consciously on the busy quay. "Thass kind on yer to tearke me on cap'n, but I wondered if yew cud find room for him an orl," he said, pointing at Jarge.

The skipper looked up. It was better than Christmas having two volunteers to serve on his ship. They must be really desperate to get to sea, he thought.

"He dun't say a lot, dew 'e," he remarked. "Mind yew, he look like he're got a honest fearce. Orl roight, he cn come on board as well an' yew cn booth find a space in the cabin."

To Jimma and Jarge the cabin bore a striking resemblance to the cell of the bridewell for its other occupant, ow Billy, was as morose and unwelcoming as the "rearpist" had been.

He was even worse that night after he had returned from his binge ashore. Jimma and Jarge slept fitfully in their bunks. Ow Billy, having taken umbrage at their intrusion into the cabin, which he regarded as his private domain, hurled abuse at them until he fell into a drunken slumber and his loud curses were replaced by even louder snoring.

Early next morning the skipper came in and Ow Billy was roused with great difficulty and much swearing. Still grumbling under his breath, he opened another hatch and disappeared from view to tinker with the engine, his expertise consisting mainly of several carefully aimed blows with a hammer. Jimma and Jarge were instructed to shovel coal.

Finally, with black smoke belching from her funnel, the Gal 'Liza slipped her moorings and chugged sluggishly through the harbour mouth and towards the open sea. To the eye of a poet or painter she would have made a brave sight, a grimy little drifter breasting the grey waves under a threatening sky.

Jimma and Jarge were unable to see the poetic aspect of the situation. Unaccustomed to the motion of the ship as she pitched and rolled in the swell which greeted her outside the harbour mouth, they began to feel decidedly queazy.

As the voyage of the Gal 'Liza towards the fishing grounds continued the weather worsened and her movements became even more unpredictable. "That might help if we hed suffin ter occupy our minds," said Jimma, looking out of the cabin hatch.

The sight which greeted him offended his landlubber's eye. "Blast if there ent a lotta water sloshin about the deck," he told Jarge. "Thet dun't half mearke the plearce look ontidy. Dew we get much more in the boot thet might sink. I reckon yew oughta git out there and mop that up."

Jarge dutifully struggled out of his bunk and took hold of the mop which Jimma held out for him, thus proving that when native cunning had been handed out he had been even further back in the queue than Jimma.

It wasn't until he had climbed out of the cabin and lurched across the deck, holding tightly to the mop, that the thought occurred to him that most of Jimma was still safely in the cabin and only his head protruded from the hatch.

Jarge just had time to think: "Idle bugger; why in't he out hare wi' me?" when a large wave swept over him and sucked him overboard.

Jimma's thought processes were even slower than usual, he being a victim of sea sickness. But even so, Jarge's sudden disappearance still registered with him as a possible emergency.

So he hauled himself through the hatch and staggered along the deck to the wheelhouse where, having been brought up to be courteous as we have already discovered, he knocked politely on the door. "Come in," yelled the skipper, followed by: "Whadd'ya want?" after Jimma had fallen into the wheelhouse.

"We're got what yer might call an emargency," gasped Jimma. "Oh ah?" said the skipper expectantly. "Yew'd better spit it out an tell me what thet is."

"Well," explained Jimma as precisely as he could under the circumstances, though not wishing to ally himself too closely to the unfortunate Jarge. "Yew know that bloke wot yew took on 'cos he hed a honest fearce."

"Yis," acknowledged the captain. "Well, he're jist buggered orf with yar mop!" exploded Jimma, full of righteous indignation.

"Dew yew mean ter say he're gorn overboard?" demanded the Captain. "Come ter think onnit, he musta done 'cos there int nowhere else fer 'im ter bugger orf tew. I know yew wus tryin ter be helpful; but why din't yew jist tell me he'd gorn over the side?"

"I jist thought the duzzy fewl shudda let go o' the mop afore he went," explained Jimma. "Thass orl I cud think of."

"I'm buggered if I din't tearke on a cuppla tules when I took on yew and 'im," said the captain. "Still, I spose we'd better dew suffin right quick ter git the mop back." Then, opening the wheelhouse window, he bawled "Billy!" into the teeth of the gale.

The sound of a man's voice could be heard thinly amid the whining of the wind. "Help," it called. "Help."

"That must be Jarge," said Jimma decisively. "That show he's out there somewhere. I hoop he're still got howd o' yar mop."

"Git yew out on deck an tie a roope round Billy's wearst," the captain told Jimma. "We'll hull 'im over the side ter look for the mop - an' that bloke as well time he's about it. At least the water'll sober 'im up"

Ow Billy's protestations were loud and long as Jimma wrestled to get the rope securely tied round his middle. "Hev yew gorn orf yar hid or suffin?" yelled Billy. But Jimma, in the heat and panic of the moment, couldn't understand why he was struggling so hard.

"Dun't yew wanta be a hero an save my meart's life?" he asked incredulously as he bundled Ow Billy over the side.

"Hev yew got howd o' the roope?" called the captain. "What roope?" shouted Jimma. "Yew din't say nothin about hangin on ter any roope!"

As luck would have it Jarge was as close to nature and all creatures great and small as any countryman could be. Like the beasts of the field, which seem to know instinctively how to swim, Jarge had managed somehow to keep his head above water.

Now he heard, rather than saw, the screaming spluttering head of Ow Billy bobbing above and beneath the waves.

Billy could swim but his expertise in the water was hampered by the fact that Jimma, when winding the rope around his body, had inadvertently pinned his arms to his sides.

"Dew I come over thare and searve yar life, will yew promise ter be in a better temper time yew git back on the boot?" shouted Jarge. "Yis, blast yer," spluttered Billy.

Thus reassured, Jarge struggled over and threw an arm under Billy's chin. And there they floated just like a pair of ducks, all serene on the surface but their feet paddling frantically below.

The captain, belatedly taking charge on board, grabbed a hefty lifebelt, tied a piece of rope round it and thrust the end into Jimma's hand. "Hull that at 'em an' hang yew onter that bloody roope," he commanded.

The lifebelt landed plumb on Billy's head thus adding concussion to his many other complaints. But Jarge was able to stick his head through the hole and hang on to Billy while Jimma and the captain hauled them back on board. The mop was never recovered.

Ow Billy was gently carried below, laid on his bunk and covered by a blanket. "Thass the fust time I're heard him bein' as quiet as this," said the captain enigmatically. "I dun't spose he're ever drunk so much water in orl his born days."

"Thass the larst time I'm a gorn ter sea," said Jarge. "I din't expect ter git sookin wet like this. My Ma'll hev suffin ter say."

"Thass sartinly the larst time yer gorn ter sea wi me, booth on yer," declared the captain, deciding on the spot to abort his fishing mission and turn for home. "One on yer's a theevin' criminal and th'other a tried to drownd my engineer."

When the Gal 'Liza returned to her humble mooring two policemen were waiting on the quay. Jimma and Jarge were led unprotestingly to the police station where Jarge's charge sheet read: "theft of one mop," and Jimma's: "aiding and abetting theft of one mop."

"I would have thought you had learned your lesson after being sent to prison for stealing those potatoes," observed the magistrate. "But it appears you didn't so you can go down for two weeks this time."

Jimma and Jarge were never to find out whether or not Ow Billy survived his one voyage in their company. Certainly his temper would not have been improved by the experience.

"I spose thass the sort o' thing what happen when yew tearke landsmen ter sea," reflected the captain as he sat back and savoured a comforting glass of rum that night.

6. The Parting of the Ways

Since a working life at sea was out of the question for Jimma, the only alternative was work on the land. And at the end of harvest there might just be time for the family to pose with one of those magnificent "troshin' engines" which powered rural life in the days of steam

Jimma and Jarge had become convinced that a life at sea was not for them. Indeed, they were beginning to wonder whether it was a good idea to venture out of their home village at all. They had only been away from it for a short time and had spent most of that in jail. They had come home branded as criminals, and had each received a good thrashing from their fathers.

"What annoy me is yew jist dun't care," said Ow Jimma. "Yew jist buggered orf wi'out so much as a by yar leave an' left me ter look arter the pigs an everythin' else.

"Yar Ma a-bin a-gorn shanny wi' worry. She're bin suffin terrible ter live with. Now yew're back agin boy yew int harf a-gorn ter hatta arn yar keep."

For Jimma, life at home was going to be difficult, to say the least. Perhaps if he and Jarge kept quiet about their brushes with the law there was still a chance they might secure jobs on one of the local farms.

So it came about that they presented themselves at the home of Farmer Greengrass and were interviewed separately in the farmhouse kitchen, Jarge first then Jimma.

It had been a forlorn hope that their adventures might have remained their secret. They had been closely questioned by their parents, and the story had inevitably got out. For a week or more it was the main topic of conversation at the Pig and Whistle.

But Farmer Greengrass was a decent man, and prepared to give any job applicant a fair hearing, especially after Ow Jimma had secretly pleaded with him: "For Heavens' searke tearke the boy on. I carn't abide him a stayin' at hoom.

"He keep a-mopin' about the plearce orl day an' th'ow gal keep a mobbin' on him about him bein' a ungreartful son. Thass even gittin' on my wick so I dun't know what thass a-doin ter him.".

Being shy and none too sure that he wanted to work for somebody else anyway, Jarge had only a brief interview with Farmer Greengrass during which very little was said. When Jimma came out into the yard after his interview Jarge asked whether they had both been taken on. "He's gorn ter give us a test," said Jimma. "He want us to go muck spreedin'. One on us a' gotta lead the hoss and the other a' gotta git up on the cart an' onlood.

"Whichever one on us dew the best job'll git tearken on. I'm a-gorn ter lead the hoss; whatta yew gorn ter dew?"

Now, even Jarge was capable of learning something from past experience, and he could just about see that Jimma had somehow taken the initiative. Jimma was not going to be quite so commited to the job as he, Jarge, would be.

He also recalled that the previous time Jimma had found him a job he had ended up swimming for his life and being accused of stealing a mop.

Somehow he sensed he was being stitched up again, and he now had this vague feeling at the back of his mind that no good would ever come to him from any job with which Jimma was in any way involved.

So he politely declined the opportunity to compete for Farmer Greengrass's favour and the two drifted apart, the friendship waning.

A great transformation came over Jarge. Now freed from the influence of Jimma he bloomed like a butterfly emerging from its chrysalis.

It was subsequently said in the village that Jarge, determined to lose his shyness by immersing himself in a life of crime, temporarily went "orf the rearls". This unjust verdict of public opinion was based on a single very public altercation which Jarge had one evening with the local constable in the village street.

Night was drawing on as Jarge cockily rode his bike past the policeman, displaying no illumination. "Where a' yar loights," called the officer authoritatively. "Somewhere near me liver!" wisecracked Jarge anatomically.

"Well yew'd better hang yar liver over yar handlebars so we cn see yer comin'," retorted the officer. It was his way of letting Jarge off with a caution - just this once.

The constable was never to understand the electrifying effect his leniency had on Jarge. Somehow, the knowledge that he had actually got away with cheeking the officer released all his inhibitions and Jarge started to become insufferably cocky.

He took a job as a milkman and was leading his horse-drawn milk float along the village street early one morning when a chance encounter brought him up with a jolt.

Miss Letitia Lavenham, a decorative young lady who aspired to a certain gentility into which she had not been born, had been having boyfriend problems.

For some time she had been exercising all her feminine wiles in the pursuit of the area's most eligible batchelor, the Hon Carleton St Peter, but he had resolutely remained unimpressed. She had lain in her lonely bed all night, unable to sleep, wrestling with her emotions and growing increasingly irritated by the lusty snoring which emanated from her parents' bedroom.

As dawn broke she flung open her bedroom window and leaned out, wearing only her flimsiest nightdress, to breathe in the fresh morning air.

The unexpected sight of Jarge plodding up the village street with the milk float suggested to her that the hour must be later than she thought. "Milkman!" she called in her most imperious voice; "Have you got the time?" "Yis my dare," responded the newly emboldened Jarge; "But who's gorn ter hold the hoss!"

Letitia immediately took offence. Jarge's enigmatic response, if it was a joke, was extremely impudent when addressed to somebody with her aristocratic ambitions. But if he, a mere milkman, really had misconstrued her innocent question as an invitation to a bedroom dalliance, then some disciplinary action had to be taken.

Her father, roused from his slumbers, was in a bad mood. Red faced and muttering under his breath, he stomped off down to the dairy to complain. Jarge got the "bullet".

The effect of this, however, was not to undermine his new-found confidence, but to convince him further that he should not work for a master. His future lay in being his own boss. Then he could behave more or less as he wanted.

So Jarge, a "late developer" in every sense, spent the rest of his life buying and selling to good effect.

His bike changed to a trade bike, from which he sold produce carefully liberated from his father's garden. Next came a van and a smallholding; then a shop, then a farm, then Government grants and the ability to employ other people to do his reading and writing for him while he kept a weather eye on the "reckoning".

Years later he and Letitia met again. Both were still single and Letitia had given up all hope of ensnaring an aristocrat. A self-made man was the next best thing, especially one rich enough to keep her in the manner to which she had always wanted to become accustomed.

"George," she said one day. "Have you got the time?" "Yis my dare," he replied again: "Hop yew inter the Rolls and we'll gorn buy a weddin' ring!"

Meanwhile, Jimma, having secured his job with Farmer Greengrass, pursued a more humble career which led, to put it briefly, from rags to rags. He secured his first job largely on the basis of Farmer Greengrass's misguided assumption that his allocation of muck spreedin jobs - "I'm a-gorn ter lead the hoss, whatta yew gorn ter dew?" - suggested a natural talent for organisation. "That boy's obviously got management potential," thought the farmer - quite inaccurately, as it turned out. "He might mearke a good hossman one day."

Having secured his employment, albeit at a modest wage and with long hours, Jimma's thoughts lightly turned to love. To be more precise, he was getting fed up with living at home with his parents. Mother, constantly reminding him of the trouble he got himself into whenever he escaped from his locked bedroom, exerted more control than ever.

And Father reasoned that the best way of keeping an eye on his son was to give him plenty of jobs to do. So every evening, when he came home from a long day's work for Farmer Greengrass, Jimma would have his tea and then find himself mucking out Father's cow house or washing down the pig sties.

Meanwhile Father, congratulating himself on finding such a character-building way of occupying Jimma's spare time, contented himself by feeding the chickens, doing his milk returns, and sitting by the kitchen fire smoking his pipe and reading the paper. He reasoned that there was no point in allocating Jimma the jobs which he liked to do himself.

Jimma's attempts to escape from the suffocating restrictions of home life began in a most unexpected way which proved that he was as innocent as ever in his dealings with the opposite sex.

At the end of one working day he was walking along the deserted country road which meandered from Farmer Greengrass's establishment to the Jimma family home when he encountered a damsel in distress.

A girl wearing cycling "bloomers" was crouching over her bicycle trying to mend a puncture. Gallantly Jimma went to her assistance.

Eventually he arrived home, red faced, agitated and an hour late for tea, to be closely questioned by his parents. "Where 'a yew bin?" demanded Father, a man in whom subtlety was not a strong point. "An' yew'd better be tellin' me the trewth dew I'll gi' yer a good larrupin, big as y'are."

"Well thass like this hare," said Jimma, overflowing with embarrassment. "I met this hare mawther what hed a bike with a puncture an' I mended it for har an' she wus ever so greartful.

"Dew yew know what?" he continued innocently. "She took me inter the woods and took orf har bloomers an laid harself down on the ground and told me I cd hev whatever I wanted. So, o' corse, I took the bike!"

"Yew did right, boy," said Father approvingly. "Arter orl, what use wud yew hev for a pair a wimmen's bloomers!"

What Jimma didn't tell Father was that, along with the girl's bike, he had also been given her name, Little Edie, and a promise to meet at the same time and place the following Wednesday.

From then on until he was found out, Jimma was late home every Wednesday, offering the excuse that he had been doing extra work for Farmer Greengrass.

In truth, it being harvest time and the stack yard being full of beautifully thatched straw stacks, Jimma and Little Edie found many a soft, straw-filled corner wherein they kissed and cuddled, and Jimma learned that when a mawther removes her bloomers she isn't necessarily offering a young lad her bike!

Discovery was awful. One Wednesday Father, having decided to check up on Jimma, went to the Greengrass farm and found no sign of him. Returning home in no good mood, he happened upon the boy and Little Edie as they emerged from the stack yard.

"I thort as much!" bawled Father angrily. "Yew're bin dewin things yew din't orta. Yew orta be ashearmed a' yarselves. Git yew orf hoom gal. An' as fer yew Jimma, yar Ma a'bin wonderin why yar clooths are all full a' straw on Wensdys. Yew'll hatta go ter bed without yar tea."

"Blast yew dew run on," cried Jimma, anxious to impress Little Edie with his boldness in standing up to his father. "Slow yew down a bit. The trewth is I wanta marry tha gal. She're bin verra kind ter me."

"Marry har?" exploded Father. "Thet ent possible. Yew're booth tew young."

"How d' yew know how owd I am?" butted in Little Edie. "Yew aren't nothin to dew wi' me!"

"We cn dew without yew stickin in yar two penn'orth," shouted Father. "I thort I told yew ter git orf hoom. Now jist hold yar duller an' sod orf!" With a sniff and a toss of her head - and a knowing wink at Jimma - Edie turned and walked off. Father took hold of Jimma's collar and began steering him in the direction of home.

As they walked, Father's mood softened and in a quiet voice, almost a whisper, he said: "This is hard to tell yer boy, but yew cudn't marry Little Edie even if yew wus old enough. The trewth is she's yar sister!

"I'd be obliged if, whenever yew wanta git married in future yew come an' talk ter me fust. Thatta'll be our little secret. I wun't tell yer Ma what yew're bin up to these Wensdys if yew dun't tell 'er what I're jist towd yew."

Jimma was dumbfounded. He was overwhelmed by the thought that his father had been occupying his spare time in a secret manner which had resulted in Jimma having relations he didn't know about.

His resolve not to tell his mother about this revealing conversation was motivated, not by a desire to avoid hurting her feelings, or to protect his Father, but by a profound wish to avoid being called a liar and given a clip round the lug.

Anyway, talking of "relations", he was horrified to think that the things he had been "up to" on those Wednesdays had been with his sister.

The exact truth was, however, that Father had been lying. His hidden purpose was to prevent Jimma from getting married so that he remained at home and available to continue doing the unpalatable jobs which Father did not enjoy.

It had to be part of the deal that Jimma was allowed a little more freedom, and a few months later he met another young girl with whom he was tempted to tie the knot. "Father," he said while muckin' out the pigs one day; "I wanta marry little ow Lucy Jones what live down the Low Road." "Blast boy," said Father. "She's another one yew can't marry. She's yar sister an' orl."

In the course of the next few years the same thing happened a number of times. Eventually Jimma, in desperation, approached his mother. "Ma," he said: "I're gotta problem."

"Yis I know, yew're allus bin a problem," she replied. "But what is it this time?"

"Well," said Jimma. "I wanta git married, but evera time I come acrorst a nice young mawther what'd set me up a treat Father say I can't wed har 'cos she's my sister. What am I gorn ter dew?"

Mother was surprisingly unmoved by this announcement. "The fust thing yew want ter dew is stop worryin' boy," she said. "Yew dun't wanta tearke no notice o' that silly owd davil; he in't no relearshun a yars!"

And this was the strange way that Jimma discovered that Father wasn't his father after all. Things were very different in the Jimma family home from that day onwards.

7. Cupid and a load of "hossmuck"

The churchyard wall was the place chosen for that historic first date between Jimma and the Gal 'Liza. As he laboriously wrote his one and only love letter, Jimma dreamed of the two of them gazing lovingly into each other's eyes.

Mawthers came and went until one day, by a curious twist of fate, Farmer Greengrass played the role of Cupid.

"His Lordship's head gardener arst me ter send a wagon lood a hossmuck fer the kitchen garden at the big house," he told Jimma. "The vegetables hen't bin doin too well up thare leartely. In fact, their cabbages a' bin more the size o' sprouts an' he think the soil need a bit a' body in it.

"Dew yew gorn lood the wagon up and hitch up ow Gypsy an' draw yew up there with it. He'll pay well."

By this time Jimma had become sufficiently trusted by Farmer Greengrass and the other farm workers to be sometimes allowed to help the "hossman" look after the fine team of working Suffolk Punches.

To his credit, Jimma loved the horses. He admired their compact rounded lines, power packed muscles, smooth golden brown coats and gentle natures. He could appreciate the symmetry of a straight furrow at ploughing time, and to understand how, as the horses moved at a powerful but steady pace, the plough followed the contours of the land.

He liked nothing better than to be asked to groom the horses and to watch their tails and manes being plaited and decorated with ribbons when Farmer Greengrass entered them at the county show.

They were proud beasts and Gypsy was the finest and most docile mare in the stables, his favourite in fact. "One day I'll hev a good ow hoss like har," he promised himself. The journey up to the hall was uneventful and Jimma, mindful of his previous visit some years before, had difficulty in resisting the temptation to leap off the waggon and ring the ornate front doorbell as Gypsy plodded towards the rear of the house.

In the walled kitchen garden Jimma and the youth who had secured the position of under gardener - mainly through having the education to keep his trousers on when interviewed by Her Ladyship - unloaded the waggon.

The head gardener, a kindly man, gave Gypsy an apple and said to Jimma: "Knock on the kitchen door an' there may be a mug o' beer for yer. Tell ow Greengrass I'll be round his ter settle up learter."

It hardly needs to be said that the kitchen door was opened by the Gal 'Liza, an older, plumper, ruddier, jollier and more confident Gal 'Liza than Jimma remembered. She had now succeeded to the position of cook and had acquired a comfortable figure not unlike a smaller version of a Suffolk Punch.

'Liza had vivid memories of Jimma's previous excursion to the big house. She peered first over his shoulder, as if looking for Jarge, and then over her own in case the butler should appear and chase Jimma off the premises again.

"Blast bor," she said. "Yew're gotta narve hen't yer, comin' hare? They're got long memories round hare an' they tell me yew're bin up to no good since I last saw yer. Gittin yarself banged up in jail. Yew don't half pong suffin high an orl."

Jimma responded to these unpromising opening remarks by ignoring the warning and explaining: "I're bin unloodin hossmuck an' the head gardener reckoned yew might hev a mug a beer for me."

"Orl right, but yew aren't comin in my kitchen wi yar bewts as dutty as they are an' pongin like yew dew," said 'Liza. "Yew'll hatta stand on the trosh'll an' drink it."

As 'Liza filled a pewter tankard with ale and cut a sizable wedge of her home-made apple pie, Jimma stood on the step and savoured the aroma of cooking which floated through the open doorway.

The pie was succulent, the ale was good and Jimma's mind was filled with pleasant thoughts as he bade "fare yer well" to 'Liza, climbed on the waggon and said: "Go on ow hoss," to Gypsy.

"Bugger me if the gal 'Liza hen't larned to cook right well," said Jimma, addressing Gypsy as there was no-one else around. "Orl this time I're bin a-lookin fer smart young floozies with pritty fearces an' well tarned ankles an' I never thought about whether they cd cook or not.

"Here a-bin 'Liza, right under my nose, fillin out nicely in orl the right plearces an' larnin harself how ter cook like that an' orl. What more cud a man want?

"Whaddya think I ort ter dew ow gal?" he asked the horse. "D'yer think I orta write har a little note and mearke an arrearngement to meet har somewhere?"

Gypsy's head nodded up and down as she plodded on, and Jimma took this as a sign of the mare's agreement that his proposed course of action was the best way to treat a woman.

With that, Jimma began thinking romantic thoughts about what he should write in the note and where they should meet. A combination of good ale, apple pie, contentment, an unusually clear conscience, the afternoon sunshine and Gypsy's sedate pace sent the contented Jimma into a deep sleep.

When he woke up a couple of hours later he was lying on the filthy floor of the wagon and could hear the sound of raised voices, one of which he recognised as that of Farmer Greengrass.

Peering over the side of the wagon he discovered that Gypsy had drawn up in front of the tap room door of the Pig and Whistle and the wagon blocked the doorway so effectively that nobody could get in or out.

Gypsy had suddenly become obstinate. There she had stopped and there she would stay. The landlord, unable either to shift Gypsy or to rouse Jimma, had sent his bottle boy to fetch Farmer Greengrass. "An' mind yew speak to Greengrass an' not ter his missus," he instructed sternly. The landlord was angry. The aroma of "hossmuck" rose from the wagon, and from Jimma. It pervaded his whole inn, filling the tap room and even rising through the bedroom windows.

Farmer Greengrass was none too happy either. It was his habit, when taking Gypsy for her regular visits to the blacksmith, or when carting hay back to the farm from outlying fields, to call in at the village pub for a pint - or two. Gypsy had stopped because this was where she was always asked to stop.

It was a habit of which Farmer Greengrass fondly believed the formidable Mrs Greengrass, a strict teetotaller and pillar of the village church, to be entirely ignorant. Now his little secret was out - or it would be if Jimma didn't keep his mouth shut!

As consciousness returned, Jimma could hear the landlord giving Farmer Greengrass a piece of his mind. "Yew wanta teach yar hoss to park yar wagon with a bit more considerearshun for others," he called loudly from the pub doorway. "My pub stink like a midden and I're got half a dozen customers stuck inside what shudda bin hoom an hour ago."

He somehow failed to mention that the pub did have a back door and that the merry sounds issuing from inside suggested that the "prisoners" were not too distraught about being incarcerated in such close proximity to all that beer.

What really bothered the landlord was that his imprisoned customers, who needed little excuse to sample his wares, had been on their way home from work and therefore had no money on them. His "slearte" was now rather longer than he would have liked.

Farmer Greengrass, red faced and apologetic, fed Gypsy a couple of carrots, coaxed her into motion and climbed up on the cart alongside Jimma.

"I won't say nothin' about this, well not this time, anyway," he said quietly. "I're lorst a coupla hours work out on yer, don't yew fergit, so y'owe me a favour which I'll remind yew about at some fewture dearte. But jist yew keep yar lip buttoned tight about the whole thing fer now, orl right?"

That night, in cottages all around the village, apologetic husbands were thinking up excuses for getting home late and smelling of beer, and were being told that their suppers had been ruined and they'd just have to like it or lump it.

Except in Jimma's house where all he had to say to Mother was: "Stop yew a mobbin' on me Ma dew I'll tell Father he in't me father and yew see if he like thet!"

After supper he found paper and pencil and retired to his bedroom. "He's up ter suffin, I'll be bound," said Father thoughtfully. But he didn't pursue the matter and thought better of reminding Jimma that the pigs needed muckin' out. They could wait until tomorrow.

In his room Jimma sat chewing his pencil for some time, wondering what to say in his note to the gal 'Liza. Finally, he began to write, slowly and carefully.

"Dare 'Liza," he wrote. "I think yew cud say we used ter be friends, but afore terday I hint sin yew for the best part of a tidy while. My hart yew're filled out nice. I was fare struck by yar bewty.

"Thet apple pie tearsted hully good an' I'd really like another slice. D'yer think we cd meet agin? How about meetin' outside the charch tomorrer at harf parst six in the evenin arter I're finished wark?

"To avoid us missin each other I'll tell yer what we can dew. If yew git there fust, an' I'm learte and yew dun't wanta hang about, dew yew put a stoon on top o the charchyard wall. If thass still thare when I git thare I'll know yew're bin an' gorn. If I git thare fust I can allus knock it orf!"

Satisfied that 'Liza would understand his tortured reasoning, Jimma signed his tentative love letter: "Respectfully Yars, Jimma", folded it and put it in an envelope addressed to The Gal 'Liza.

That night he slipped quietly out of the house and headed across the fields to the hall. All was in darkness as he crept around the back.

A chain rattled, a threatening shape rose out of the darkness. The dog barked and growled threateningly. A light came on upstairs.

Quickly Jimma thrust his letter under the kitchen door. The dog was going frantic now and lights were coming on all over the house.

Jimma fled. The great front door opened, and for the second time in his life Jimma was running along the drive hotly pursued by the butler.

Round the back in the kitchen, the gal 'Liza, her hair in curlers and a coat hastily flung over her voluminous red flannellette nightdress, looked anything but "bewtiful" as she picked up Jimma's note from the kitchen floor and hid it in her ample bosom.

The door opened and in came the butler, clad in pyjamas, his face red, his normally immaculate hair dishevelled and his chest heaving with the exertion of the chase.

"Are you all right?" he inquired breathlessly. "Yis, I'm orl right," said the gal 'Liza. "I think thare a-bin an intrewder in the kitchen garden. Some pore hungry soul arter suffin t'eat, peraps. But thare int nothin missin an' no harm's bin dun so go yew back ter bed." At that moment the voice of the new chambermaid wafted sweetly down the back stairs which led to the servants' bedrooms. "Hurry up Henry; I'm gittin cold up hare all alone," it said.

The butler's face grew even more flushed. "Well, so long as you are sure everything is in order I will do as you say," he muttered and retreated hurriedly back upstairs.

The gal 'Liza took Jimma's letter out of her bosom, smiled a knowing little smile and went back to her bedroom to read it.

8. Till Death Us Dew Part

"Blast gal, yew wanta give a bloke a bit o' warnin' afore yew creep up ahind him an' yell in his lug. I'm alookin' fer that stoon yew wus s'posed ter hev left on the wall."
"How c'd I put a stoon on the wall when I hent bin hare yit?"

While life had dealt kindly with the Gal 'Liza in the sense that she had never been hungry and had always been in employment, it had not brought her much in the way of romance.

Her culinary skills had secured her promotion to cook at the big house, but she sometimes hankered for the time when, as a young mawther, she had been such an object of desire in the village that she could afford to spurn the advances of an awkward youth like Jimma.

"'Liza had been a restless soul in those days, "walking out" with one well scrubbed and hopeful beau after another. Even that nice softly spoken young man who had taken a shine to her after getting the under-gardener's job that Jimma had wanted did not last long.

Her father had become so tired of the many lovesick swains who came knocking at his door and asking for 'Liza that he had decided his best course of action was to find her a job which kept her busy, fed her and supplied a roof over her head - preferably somebody else's roof.

So 'Liza went into service at the big house. She was only seen at her family home once a week on her afternoon off. Her mother was less happy with this arrangement than her father.

A domineering man who tended to get aggressive when drunk, he said: "Hard wark never hart no-one an' thet 'ont dew the gal 'Liza no harm ter see how the Quality live."

For 'Liza, the opportunity to see how the "Quality" lived had not particularly endeared them to her. She very quickly realised that their comfortable lifestyle depended entirely on the hard work of the ordinary folk.

The long working day, along with Her Ladyship's unwaveringly strict rule that the servants were not allowed to receive gentleman callers, meant that there had been very few opportunities for 'Liza to consort with the opposite sex.

So she had compensated by making sure that she sampled more than her fair share of the dishes prepared in her own kitchen, and had, in consequence, grown plump.

All this, and the absence of better alternatives, tempted her to look with favour on the one and only love letter that Jimma ever wrote - or that she had ever received, for that matter.

All right, so "iggerance" had deprived him of a job at the big house, but who wanted to work there anyway?

Also in his favour was the fact that he had travelled to foreign parts, seeing wonderful things that she hadn't seen. He'd been as far as Lowestoft, after all, and she vaguely remembered somebody once telling her that travel broadened the mind. Praps one day she'd be able to go to Lowestoft.

The rest of the young men with whom she had come into contact had stayed local, so she believed, and were unlikely to know anything of the great wide world which lay beyond the boundaries of the village.

Perhaps Jimma had left the village a boy and come back a man. A girl could always hope so, anyway.

He had also been to jail - twice. Oh yes, her father would tell her that people who went to prison were no better than they should be.

But the experience also lent a touch of mystery to the man, and perhaps there was an adventurous spark somewhere deep in 'Liza's soul which gave her the wish to live dangerously!

So 'Liza decided to keep her date with destiny at the churchyard wall. But, in order not to appear too eager, she resolved to arrive ten minutes late.

The first sight she had of Jimma was of his unattractive rear end. He was crouching on all fours at the foot of the wall scrabbling about in the grass with his hands.

"What are yew a-dewin on?" asked 'Liza from just behind Jimma's elevated posterior. He whirled round, accidentally banging his head on the wall.

"Yew wanta be careful dewin things like thet," said 'Liza sympathetically. "That wall's hundreds of yare owd. Thass a ancient monument and gittin a bit fragile. The last thing that want is hevin yar hid bangin inter it."

"Blast gal, yew wanta give a bloke a bit of warnin afore yew creep up ahind 'im an' yell in his lug," complained Jimma, rubbing the side of his head ruefully.

"I din't yell," disputed 'Liza. "Anyway, what are you a-dewin on?"

"I'm a-lookin fer thet stoon yew wus sposed ter hev left on the wall," said Jimma.

"I din't put no stoon on no wall," said 'Liza. "How cud I a put a stoon on the wall when I hen't bin here yit? I're only jist arrived."

"Bugger me, I never thought a that," said Jimma. "If yew'll pardon my langwidge. I never thought about me bein the fust one hare.

"Come ter think onnit, thass lucky we met, ent it; we cud easily a-missed one another wi yew not bein' hare to put yar stoon on the wall.

"That must be fearte. I reckon we wus fearted ter meet, come what may. We musta bin mearde fer each other, yew an' me!"

'Liza, unable to see the logic of Jimma's argument, was nevertheless prepared to consider its conclusion favourably. Whilst she did not necessarily accept that she and Jimma had been "mearde fer each other", she could at least view the prospect of a lifetime spent in his company as being preferable to continued employment at the big house where she would undoubtedly end up an embittered old maid.

So she decided to move their blossoming relationship on a little. Fishing in her coat pocket she brought out a large piece of apple pie wrapped in a cloth. It was a gesture of good will which further convinced Jimma that they were soul mates.

A lifetime's access to that apple pie was as close as Jimma's limited imagination could get to Paradise. He looked longingly at 'Liza as he bit into the pie. "Oh 'Liza!" he said, chewing appreciatively and spitting out a clove as decorously as he could, for he knew his manners. "Oh Jimma!" she responded with affection.

This monosyllabic exchange was the first of many as Jimma and 'Liza met regularly in the shade of the old churchyard wall and stared longingly into each other's eyes. Their inability to think of anything else to say at least offered the promising prospect of a peaceful marriage.

Jimma ventured to put his arm round 'Liza's shoulder and lent her his hat when it rained. She responded by keeping him more than adequately supplied with apple pie.

"D'yer think we shud git hitched?" said Jimma one day. "I'll think about it," responded 'Liza, knowing that marriage would be her only escape from the big house but relishing the chance to play hard to get.

A week later she greeted him with the announcement: "The answer's yis."

"What was the question?" asked Jimma, momentarily nonplussed. "Oh blast yis, I remember now. My hart gal, yew're mearde me very 'appy. I spose yew sayin yis mean we're engearged. I'll hatta go hoom an' tell my ow ma and pa that yew're now my intended." "Howd yew hard a minnit," cautioned 'Liza. "I hen't arst my father's permission yit."

It would be an exaggeration to say that both sets of parents were delighted by the news. Both mothers thought their offspring could have done better in the marriage stakes. Jimma's father strongly objected on the grounds that his son would be setting up house with 'Liza and would no longer be available to do those odd jobs around the yard.

And the engagement was a great disappointment to 'Liza's father who had been happy with the thought that if his daughter remained single he wouldn't have to pay for a wedding breakfast, the rest of his several children being sons.

"I wish yew'd a-bin born a boy," he told 'Liza when she dutifully asked for his approval of the union. "I aren't so much losin' a daughter as gainin a lotta friends what I din't know I hed, an' they'll all want feedin.

"Anyway, I reckon if yew hatta git hitched at all, yew mighta tried a bit harder ter find somebodda better'n 'im.

"Still, if yew must I spose yew will, an' I cn allus kill a pig so we cn give 'em all a bit o' cold ham."

Up at the hall Her Ladyship gave a sigh of resignation when the butler told her that 'Liza was leaving to get married. "Good cooks don't grow on trees," she remarked. "And we've just trained the girl up, too."

"Will we need to advertise for a new one - or does the new chambermaid include cooking among her many undisclosed talents?" she asked with an arched eyebrow.

The butler became confused. This faintest of hints that Her Ladyship knew more than he had fondly believed about his secret dalliances with the housemaid was enough to ruffle even the most urbane of family retainers.

"Er, I don't know, Your Ladyship," he said hesitantly. "I shall have to ask her."

"Perhaps you could raise the subject when you meet later on tonight. . . . . . ." - Her Ladyship left the statement hanging in the air like a thinly veiled rebuke.

"Have you heard who it is that Cook is marrying, Your Ladyship?" asked the butler, anxious to change the subject. "One of those ignorant young fools who dropped their trousers when you interviewed them for a job."

"Good heavens," exclaimed Her Ladyship. "In that case I am glad Cook is leaving. I have no wish to employ somebody who shows such poor judgment! She can leave at once, whether the chambermaid can cook or not!"

Jimma and 'Liza, and both their families, were in church to hear the banns read, and both fathers had to be forcibly restrained from standing up when Canon Gunn invited interventions from anybody who "knew just cause or impediment why these two should not be joined in Holy Matrimony."

The wedding day was sunny, the guests resplendent in their Sunday suits, summer frocks and best hats. Villagers who had not been invited stood round the lych gate studying the fashions, discussing the guests and casting a critical eye over the bride.

"I aren't one ter spread gossip," said one village housewife with a knowing wink at her neighbour. "But they dew say she dun't orta be a-wearin white. She in't ser innersent as she like ter mearke out!"

Canon Gunn delivered a thunderous sermon on sex being a gift of God, approved only for married couples and specifically intended for the procreation of children, and not for the gratification of Man's carnal desires which were a gift of the devil himself.

Most of the congregation, looking at the Canon's thin, hard faced and haughty wife, felt they could understand why he took this view.

The hymns were inspiring. With the prim Winifred Bell performing an error-strewn accompaniment on those notes of the church's decrepit pipe organ from which any sound could be coaxed, the congregation raised their voices joyfully in "Fight the Good Fight" and "Through the Night of Doubt and Sorrow."

After these appropriately doom laden hymns the 23rd psalm added a bit of light relief by leading them through the valley of death. They liked the tune.

The wedding breakfast was held in the upstairs room at the Pig and Whistle. The speeches were short. Jimma could think of nothing to say.

Farmer Greengrass, as best man, was waxing eloquent on the theme that "marriage is an institution but, given the choice, no-one in their right mind would live in an institution," when he received the full blast of a withering glare from his wife, and promptly sat down.

The bride's father almost provoked a punch-up. Fortified by liberal quantities of brown ale to wash down the cold ham, he stood up and proposed a toast to the happy couple.

"May orl yar trubbles be littl'uns," he joked in time honoured fashion. Hugely amused at his own wit, he added a word of advice. "Doon't expect them trubbles ter git smaller as the kids git bigger. Tha only thing what happen is the datty finger marks go higher up the wall."

All would have been well if he had left it at that. But he had to add an afterthought. "Mind yew," he said pointedly: "I can't think why my daughter din't look round a bit harder afore she lit on that bloke. She cudda dun better'n 'im."

Jimma's mother rose in righteous defence of her son. "Are yew incinereartin my son en't much of a catch?," she asked, determined to prove she could use posh words if she set her mind to it.

"Jist look at 'im," retorted 'Liza's father, his voice becoming increasingly slurred and argumentative. "Anybodda cn see that even if 'is lamps are lit thare ent nobody at hoom! Yew musta hed a funny ow midwife when he wus born. She musta slung away the bearby an' kep' the afterbarth, if yer arst me!"

"Nobody arst yew!" retorted Jimma's mother. "My son ent daft, he only look it. Though come ter think onnit, he must be a bit sorft in tha hid ter git cort up wi' yar family."

Then turning to her husband, she added: "Aren't yew gorn ter dew nothin about this mortal offence what he're give ter yar son? Are yew a man or an ow hin?"

Stung by this challenge, Father rose majestically, if a trifle unsteadily, from his seat. He had also sampled the brown ale to excess. Ponderously he raised his fists. "Which one on yer want a clip round the lug?" he demanded aggressively.

Jimma and the gal 'Liza did not hang around to find out. Their honeymoon was to be a week in Lowestoft - 'Liza had heard of Jimma's adventures there and wanted to see the place for herself.

So, as confusion reigned in the top room of the Pig and Whistle, they sneaked out unnoticed and went home to change.

As a wedding present to themselves they had bought a tandem bike which was to be their conveyance to Lowestoft. Jimma took the front seat and steered, 'Liza took it easy at the back.

As they passed the Pig and Whistle on their way out of the village the sounds of revelry could be heard. But they noticed that the village policeman's bicycle was leaning against the front wall. Evidently the law had been called in to restore order.

Now the two families had forgotten their differences and a good party was in progress. There would be many hangovers in the village next morning.

A man's voice rose above the general hubbub. "Drink up, whatya gorn ter hev, all on yer!" it shouted.

The Gal 'Liza was almost certain that the voice was that of her father, but she could not be entirely sure since it sounded somewhat muffled, as if delivered from under the table, and she had never heard him make that speech before.

Anyway, she was not going to hang around now, even if he did feel disposed to make it again.

An hour later the tandem slowed to a halt and Jimma got off, bent down and let the air out of the front tyre.

"'Liza looked at him in mild surprise. "What the davil did yer dew that for?' she asked. "Well thass so's I cn reach the pedals easier," Jimma explained affably.

"'Liza decided she would never be able to understand her new husband's thought processes. It seemed blindingly obvious to her that what he had just done was stupid.

So she also alighted from the bike, took a small spanner out of the bag and removed the rear set of handlebars and seat.

Jimma stood back and watched intently as 'Liza replaced the handlebars where the seat had been and the seat in the hole reserved for the handlebars.

"What the hell are yew a-doin on gal," demanded the bemused Jimma. "Well," replied 'Liza: "If yew're gorn ter act so sorft, sayin yew carnt reach the pedals, I'm a gorn hoom!"

The two remounted the bike, facing in opposite directions. "Thiss in't no good," declared Jimma. "I still carnt reach the pedals. We'll hatta walk and push th'ow bike to the nearest pub an see if they're gotta room for the night."

The gal 'Liza looked admiringly at Jimma. "Blast I think I done right in a-marryin yew arter orl," she said. "I bet there ent no problem wot git yew down. I reckon thass 'cos yew're travelled an' sin a bit o' the warld!"

An hour later the newly weds, tired and dusty, walked up to the door of a wayside inn. Yes, the landlord assured them, he actually had two spare rooms, and since he doubted very much their story that they were married they would have to pay for them both and sleep separately.

Late that night, as Jimma lay in his lonely bed wondering if this was really what married life should be like, his bedroom door creaked open and he could dimly see a well rounded shape creeping quietly in.

The covers were pulled back, the bedsprings creaked and Jimma felt the comforting touch of flannellette against his skin.

Turning towards the new arrival he stretched out his arm and said, with relief and deepest affection: "Oh 'Liza!"

An arm encircled him in a hug which almost took his breath away. "Oh Jimma," whispered a familiar voice in his ear. Married life had begun.

9. On Building a Home and a Family

Farmer Greengrass was a wise and kindly man. Not only did he allow Ow Hinry to stay in his cottage next door to Jimma and the Gal 'Liza, but he would also help his tenant by cutting the hedge and doing other odd jobs.

The cottage which Farmer Greengrass had set aside for Jimma and 'Liza was only sparsely furnished, and after several months of hard saving they decided to go to the nearest town to buy some chairs. "I dun't want any ow rubbish, even though we are hard up," said Jimma. "You want stuff ter last. I fancy some o' them anteeks if they dun't corst tew much."

"My Father allus reckon yew carnt dew better than a good anteek," he said, warming to his subject. "They're owd and they're well mearde an' yew c'n allus find ways a-mearkin' 'em larst a bit longer.

"Father ha got a ow anteek in his shud. Thass his pride an' joy. Thass a owd axe, an' thatta bin handed down in our family fer generearshuns.

"Thass so owd Father're hed ter fit two knew hids and three new handles in the time he're had it, so goodness know how many thet hed to hev afore thet come ter 'im!"

Jimma having thus expressed himself, with unusual eloquence, on his preferences by way of furniture, he and 'Liza got down to the job of making arrangements for their trip to the nearest market town.

Farmer Greengrass, a kindly man at heart, agreed to lend them Gypsy and the wagon - "on condition yew dunt fall asleep while yew're a-drivin', Jimma" - and they headed for town.

The journey was going well, the horse plodding amiably along. The sun was shining and the young couple were peacefully admiring the countryside and the crops when suddenly Canon Gunn swept round a corner ahead of them, driving his new car.

There were few cars on the roads of East Anglia in those days, and only two in Jimma's village. One belonged to the local doctor and the other to the Vicar whose parochial stipend - in the gift of Lord Wymond-Hayme as patron of the living - was supplemented by his own private means.

Canon Gunn's vehicle was his pride and joy, an expensive toy in which he careered around the district at breakneck speed. Many were the hair raising stories of the near-death experiences suffered by villagers after encountering the Canon in his car.

The country roads were far too narrow and twisty for vehicles propelled by what Jimma's father always called "the infarnal combustion engine".

The sudden appearance of the car unnerved Gypsy. Never having seen such a fast and fearsome beast before, she stopped, rooted to the spot, as the vehicle swerved across the road ahead then back to its own side.

With two wheels mounting the grass bank it rushed past the horse and cart with inches to spare. "Sorry!" bawled the Canon gaily as he disappeared into the distance.

But Jimma and 'Liza were far too busy to hear his apology. Gypsy had set off as if ejected by a spring. She was now proceeding at a far from sedate gallop with Jimma hanging on to the reins as if his life depended on his never leaving go - which it did.

As the wagon hurtled around a corner the gal 'Liza, clinging to the side with one hand and to her hat with the other, shrieked: "I'd give ten pounds ter be outa here!"

"Dun't yew worry gal," screamed Jimma, struggling for some semblance of control over the fleeing horse: "Yew'll be outa here fer nothin' in a minnit."

His prophecy came true as they passed the very next farmyard. As Gypsy charged past the farm entrance the waggon hit a rut in the road and 'Liza left the vehicle quite unintentionally.

Her momentum took her over the hedge - and head first into a gently steaming heap of "hossmuck".

The effect on Gypsy was instant. It was as if 'Liza's departure from the cart had been her objective all along and, having achieved it, she could now relax. The look of panic in her eyes was replaced by one of mischief.

She stopped abruptly. Jimma didn't. He tumbled over the front of the wagon and suddenly found himself clinging desperately to Gypsy's ample bottom.

He slid down on to the road and, as Gypsy turned and bent her head to graze at the roadside, Jimma walked back to the place where his wife had inadvertently abandoned ship.

Nothing could be seen of the gal 'Liza except her well shined button boots sticking out of the muck heap and waving about frantically. From deep within the steaming pile came 'Liza's muffled cries for help.

Jimma took a firm grip on the boots and pulled hard. The rest of 'Liza emerged, her long skirt riding up to display her bloomers to any chance passer by.

Her face was red with embarrassment, exertion, fright and the heat of the innermost recesses of the heap. "I'll dew fer thet thare Vicar dew he drive like that thare agin, I'll dew fer 'im, yew see if I dornt," she shouted.

"An' yew might a-dun a bit better controllin that thare hoss, Jimma. I're hart myself an' yew dunt care a sight. That ent leardylike to hev ter be dragged outer a muck heap feet fust an' showin' yar bloomers. Yew dunt know who mighta bin a-gorn past."

Liza continued in this vein for some minutes while desperately trying to straighten her clothing and remove vestiges of hossmuck and straw from her person.

"I dunt know what yew're runnin on about," said Jimma with a noticeable lack of sympathy. "Arter all, that wus a sorft landin an yew only went in up ta yer ankles!"

Liza's punch landed on Jimma's left ear and he was still seeing stars as she walked back up the road, climbed into the wagon and sat down. "Well?" she demanded. "Are yew a-gorn ter tearke me hoom or what?"

"What," said Jimma. It wasn't a question but a statement. "We're so near the town now we might as well carry on ter the farniture shop. We dew need them chairs."

"Yew dunt want ter think I'm a-gorn inter no shop smellin' like this," said 'Liza.

But they carried on into town, and while Jimma went into the shop 'Liza stayed outside, sitting self consciously in the wagon and getting some sideways glances from passing "townies" who made audible comments to each other about bumpkins from out in the sticks smelling like cess pits.

Inside the shop Jimma addressed the man behind the counter. "I want a coupla chairs, if yer dun't mind, an' I'd like ter hev a look at yar anteeks."

"Right away, sir. Follow me," answered the shop assistant, leading the way into a large store room at the back of the shop. A narrow pathway led between two large piles of assorted furniture into which the assistant dived with enthusiasm.

Lifting out the odd chair or table, mostly of a quality which even Jimma recognised as "old" rather than "antique", he began to wear a puzzled expression.

"I know I hed a coupla anteeks somewhere," he muttered. "But I musta jist misleard 'em fer a minnit. Would yew kindly mind a-weartin in the shop time I rummage around a bit more?"

Jimma returned to the outer shop and waited while lumps and crashes and muffled swearing issued from the back room. Eventually the door opened and the assistant returned, staggering under the weight of a large heavy wooden chair with long straight back and corkscrew legs.

"Thare y'are!" he announced, his face flushed but triumphant. "Whadda ya think a thet. Thatta got all the signs of a real anteek, thet hev. Dark wood, bandy legs, wunnerful carvin' and proper authentic warm holes.

"An' dun't yew worry; I're got another one jist like that back thare," he added, indicating the store room door. "Yew c'n hev the pair."

"Ah," said Jimma, determined to drive a hard bargain. "That may look like a anteek but how c'n I be sure thet really is a anteek? Thet could be a fearke what yew knocked tergather in yar back yard. Yew cudda put them warm hools in thare with a little ow' gimlet."

The assistant was ready to take umbrage, until he remembered that the shop owner had insisted most sternly that, however sorely he was provoked and however daft the customer might appear, that customer was always right.

"I'll ignore thet larst remark," he said. "Meantime, dew yew jist look hare, under the seat. Thatta got two letters, 'Q.A.' That mean that wus mearde in the reign o' Queen Anne."

"That dunt mean nothin o' the sort," replied Jimma, determined to show he was not as daft as he looked and had absorbed some small knowledge of British history from Mr Swishem.

"On a door ter a little ow shud I're got in my garden at hoom thatta got the letters 'W.C.', but even I know that dunt mean ter say, thet wus mearde in the reign o' Willum the Conkerer!"

"Maybe not,' countered the shop assistant, drawing on his superior knowledge of antiques. "But if yew want further proof thet this hare chair is the genuine article, jist yew look at the legs. Queen Anne's legs is allus thick an' bandy."

Jimma had to admit that history lessons at the village school had never covered the shape or configuration of Queen Anne's legs, so he was obliged to give ground.

"Orl right then," he said. "How much dew yer want fer the pair?"

"I reckon if I arst yew nineteen shillins an' elevenpence ha'penny each I'm a-givin' on-'em away," said the shop assistant. "But thass what yew c'n hev 'em for, seein as how yew dunt look well enough britched ter pay more."

"Blast," said Jimma, with feeling: "Yew dunt half drive a hard bargain." But he paid up and the shop assistant helped him carry the chairs out and load them into the cart, sniffing the air as he did so, and giving 'Liza a puzzled look.

Seated side by side on their new chairs, Jimma holding the horse's reins, the young couple looked quite regal as they started their homeward journey.

The shop assistant watched them disappear round the corner. "I wunder if I shudda just mentioned ter that fella, quietly like, thet his missus ha got a parsonal hygiene problem," he thought. "Thet mighta bin the kind thing ter dew. Maybe he dunt notice it. Mind yew, she did hev the decency ter stay outa the shop."

Then he turned, went back through the shop and the store-room and into the yard. Drawing a key from his waistcoat pocket, he unlocked the door of a large shed.

From within he withdrew two chairs identical to the ones he had just sold Jimma. Shoving them into the store room, he said to himself: "The guvnor like ter hev plenty o' anteeks in stock. I'll hatta suggest he git young Charlie ter mearke a couple more."

At about this time Jimma and 'Liza were passing Sarah's cottage on their way home. Sarah, standing outside the open door, called: "Yew tew look like the King an' Queen o' England settin' up thare on yar throons."

"There's a big difference 'twin me an' the Queen," 'Liza called back. "She probly wear a better class o' hossmuck."

Mystified, Sarah turned to go into her cottage. "That gal shudda paid heed ter what my ow Ma used ter say," she thought. "Dew yew carnt thinka nothin sensible ter say, dunt say nothin' at all."

10. A Hoss of My Own

"Be diplomatic when yew're a meetin' a cow called Gertrude for the fust time" Ow Jimma had told his son. "They loike ter be torked tew perlitely".

"Seein' as how that boy ent at hoom no more ter help me out wi' the chores, he need suffin ter dew ter occupy his spare time." It was Ow Jimma talking.

"I dun't spose he're gotta lotta spare time," said Mother. "Farmer Greengrass keep him busy and when he git hoom I reckon the Gal 'Liza'll hev plenty o' little jobs lined up fer him ter dew, if she're got any sense."

Young Jimma and the Gal 'Liza were busy setting up their home. Their efforts to make the place look homely and familiar received an unexpected boost one day, by courtesy of their neighbour, Ow Hinry, who had worked on the farm all his life and now did odd jobs around the place.

Ow Hinry, a bachelor, had been a willing worker, though not a particularly able one even in his prime. Farmer Greengrass, a kindly and generous man, had never had the heart to get rid of him and throw him out of his home.

So Ow Hinry stayed put in the cottage which adjoined the new home of Jimma and 'Liza. Well into his eighties, he was a colourful country character full of wise sayings which meant very little on account of his not having very much common sense to back them up.

Farmer Greengrass's daughter Deirdre had taken a liking to the old man. A talented artist, she had sketched him as he pottered about the farmyard, and had produced a rather romanticised portrait of the old man in oils.

One afternoon she visited Ow Hinry in his cottage and presented him with the picture with great ceremony.

"Blast, ent that nice," said Ow Hinry appreciatively. "I're got the very plearce ter hang that up in my bedrume. Then when I wearke up evera mornin' I'll see meself lookin' back at me an' I'll know I int dead yit."

Deirdre was glad the old man liked his gift, even if she had difficulty following his logic. As soon as she had gone Ow Hinry went out to his shed, found a hammer and a large nail, and took the picture upstairs.

What the old man didn't realise, as he hammered the nail into the wall, was that the nail was six inches long and the wall only four inches thick.

That night, as Jimma and the Gal 'Liza undressed for bed, 'Liza let out a cry of surprise.

Jimma, modestly turning his back and putting his long nightshirt on before removing his long johns, was alarmed. "I hoop yew din't see suffin yew din't ort tew," said the innocent young bridegroom."'Corse not," answered 'Liza. "D'yer think if I hedda dun I'd a sounded so surprised. Yew hent got nothin' I hent sin afore!"

Jimma was prepared to overlook this enigmatic revelation. "Then why did yew holler out like that?" he asked.

"Well there's a duzzy grit ow nearle come threw the bedrume wall. That wun't there this mornin'."

Together the young couple pondered this new development. True, they could complain to Ow Hinry, but on the other hand, this nail could have been an omen sent from above.

For, leaning against their bedroom wall was a heavy old fashioned picture frame containing a fading portrait of 'Liza's Great Aunt Gertrude.

Liza remembered her late great aunt as a formidable, stern and dictatorial old spinster who had worn black from neck to ankles, and whose spartan and uncomfortable home 'Liza had often been obliged to visit as a young girl.

Great Aunt Gertrude was held in awe by 'Liza's mother who had given her the portrait as a wedding gift, and had advised her: "Whatever yew dew, gal, dew yew find a plearce on yar bedrume wall fer Aunt Gertrude. Where-ever she is now the ow gal'll be a-wantin' ter keep har eye on yew ter mearke sure yew dunt git up ter nothin unseemly in yar private lives. She never did loike smut."

Amid all their furniture removals Jimma and 'Liza had not been able to agree where Great Aunt Gertrude should be hung. Ow Hinry's nail, they concluded, must have been a meaningful hint from the spirit world.

From that moment the old lady's disapproving glare was the last thing Jimma and 'Liza felt as they fell innocently asleep at night, and the first thing they saw when they woke up in the morning.

It effectively stifled even the remotest chance that the pure young couple might indulge in even the most tentative efforts to procreate.

Meanwhile, all the innocent home building activity in which Young Jimma and the gal 'Liza were indulging did not alter Ow Jimma's view that his son still had spare time on his hands.

"Yew wanta dew loike everybody else dew an' keep a few animals," he told Young Jimma one day. "Chickens, a pig and a cow to provide eggs, bearcon and milk fer the house."

"I sorta fancied keepin' a few goots," said Jimma. "They're easy ter feed an' I dunt mind a drop a goot's milk now an' agin."

"Goots int no good, boy," said Father. "Yew hint got nowhere ter put' em in the winter."

"Well, I cud allus keep 'em in the bedrume time I'm a-buildin' on-'em a shelter," protested Jimma.

"Yew cud dew, I spose," agreed Father. "But what about the smell?"

"Oh thass orl right," responded Jimma. "Goots ent any tew particlar; they'll hatta put up with that!"

Jimma never did keep goats in his bedroom. The Gal 'Liza put her foot down with a firm hand. "And anyway," she explained: "Great Aunt Gertrude would never approve!"

But he did acquire chickens, a cow called Gertrude (out of respect), and a sow for which Jimma and his father built a comfortable sty.

Even then he was not satisfied. He had always enjoyed looking after Gypsy and thought it would be nice to have a horse of his own. So one day he caught the train for Norwich where he had heard there was a good livestock market.

It was the first of several visits he was unexpectedly to make to the city centre market which stood in the shadow of the ancient Norman castle, sitting proudly on its man-made mound.

Livestock pens covered the market area and business was brisk as the farmers followed the auctioneers from one pen full of animals to another.

Jimma's route towards the market took him past a row of shops, one of which was a pet shop outside which a gaudy coloured parrot sat on a perch.

As Jimma walked past the parrot said, in a broad East Anglian accent: "I know yew!"

Jimma looked hard at the bird, turned round and walked past it again. Again it said: "I know yew."

Jimma was intrigued, but at that moment he had other things on his mind. Out of the corner of his eye he spotted two farm horses tethered to a rail. One, a Suffolk mare which looked as if it had seen better days during a hard working life, reminded Jimma of Gypsy.

Trade had been slow for the horse dealer who was sitting on a bench nearby, apparently asleep. He leapt immediately into action when Jimma approached and patted the Suffolk.

"Hallo ow gal," Jimma whispered in its ear. "D'yer reckon yew'd loike ter come hoom longa me? I 'ont wark yer tew hard. I only really want yer as a pet."

The old horse turned its head and fixed Jimma with a soulful gaze. It was as if she was saying: "Take me away from all this. I'll be yours for life."

He was already won over by the beast's mute eloquence before the horse dealer swung smoothly into his sales pitch.

"What a foine animile," he said. "Sound in wind an' limb an' a luvly set o' fetlocks. What more cud any man want. She's called Nelly. Are yer reddy ter mearke me an offer?"

Jimma made a modest offer which, to his surprise, was immediately accepted without argument. Then man and horse set off on the long walk home.

Later that morning over a cup of tea in the nearby market cafe. the horse dealer told his friends: "I're jist sold ow Nelly agin. I wus beginnin' ter think she wus gittin tew owd fer this gearme an' wud hev ter go ter the knacker's."

There were frequent stops for the horse to graze at the roadside, and an overnight stay with Nelly tethered to a five barred gate and Jimma sleeping under a hedge.

They arrived at their destination during the evening of the next day. Exhausted but happy, Jimma let the horse loose in the meadow and went off to bed.

He was awakened early next morning by the agitated voice of the gal 'Liza. "That ow hoss dunt look nun tew sharp," she said, breathless from running upstairs to the bedroom. "Thass a-lyin' there lookin' a bit white round the gills."

Jimma scrambled into some clothes and rushed out to the meadow. The horse was lying very still and cold. The vet was called and confirmed that the poor animal was dead.

Jimma was devastated. All his life he had wanted a horse of his own and now, just as he had achieved that ambition, a cruel fate had snatched it away.

His one consolation was that, in death, old Nelly's face seemed to be wearing a gentle secret smile. She had, at least, cheated the knacker. Perhaps that had been her ambition.

Next day Jimma was back on the train heading for Norwich Market. Somewhat to his surprise the horse dealer was there again. He made straight for the man.

"Yew know that hoss what yew sold me th'other day," he said indignantly.

"I may dew, and then agin I may not," said the horse dealer, not wishing to commit himself until he knew what had happened. "That depend on whether I c'n recall yar fearce, an' whether I did sell yew a hoss, or whether I sold another hoss ter another bloke. Thass true I did sell a hoss th'other day, but then I sell hosses most days. Anyway, wass up?"

"Well that poor ow bugger ha' keeled over, tarned up its heels and died," said Jimma, admitting that he did not know much about horses but he knew enough to realise it should not have done that.

"Bugger me!" exclaimed the horse dealer. "Yew're roight, that shunt ha' dun that. That hent never dun that afore!"

"'Corse the bugger hent never dun that afore!" shouted Jimma. "That cud only peg out once, yer sorft tule."

"What I meant wus that dunt usually peg out, that usually git out o' the medder an' mearke its way back ter my plearce so I c'n sell it again," explained the horse dealer helpfully. "I're mearde a lotta money outa ow Nelly's hoomin' instinct.

"Thass a bit loike one o' them pigeons only that walk hoom instead o' flyin'. Mind yew, I dunt spose I shudda towd yew that, but that dunt mearke a sight a difference now she's dead."

"Anyway," he continued, stifling Jimma's increasingly heated protests. "Yew carn't hev yar money back 'cos orl we did wus shearke hands on the deal. I never writ out a bit o' pearper an' yew never signed nothin'. Dew yew hint got nothin down in black an' white yew hint got no proof yew ever bought a hoss at all."

"Yew theevin' ow varmint," shouted Jimma, throwing a punch in the horse dealer's direction. The latter did a smart side-step and Jimma, off balance, collided with the rear end of a startled shire horse which, with an equally nifty bit of footwork, planted our hero flat on his back in the mud.

"Yew better shove orf dew I'll call the police an' git yew had up fer assault an' battery," threatened the horse dealer. Jimma, knowing he was on a hiding to nothing, decided to cut his losses. A third term in prison was definitely not a good idea.

He was walking away from the scene of his humiliation when a sharp crackly voice cut into his thoughts. "I know yew," it said.

Jimma turned, startled. The parrot was sitting on its perch fixing him with a flinty eye. "I know yew," it repeated.

"Shut yew up," said Jimma, still sore. He moved away, but despite himself, he was intrigued by this knowing bird. He wanted a pet and wouldn't a talking parrot be at least as much company as a horse, and a good deal more colourful?

He turned back and entered the shop, the parrot's knowing voice following him inside.

"That parrot yew're got outside," he said to the old man behind the counter. "How much dew yer want fer it?"

The man sucked his teeth and shook his head. "I'm sorry ow partner," he said with genuine regret. "I carn't possibly sell him. He's far tew valuable. He know tew much.

"Tell yer what I'll dew though. I'll dew yer a fair deal. I carn't sell yer the parrot hisself but I'll sell yer three of his eggs. A fiver each'd be a fair price.

"Orl yew're gotta dew is tearke 'em hoom and stick 'em in the oven, stook up the fire a bit, an' they'll sune hatch out. Then, fer fifteen quid yew'll hev three o' them intelligent parrots for the price o' one an' yew c'n sune teach 'em orl ter talk."

Jimma took the eggs home and did as the man had instructed. Soon the flutter of tiny wings was heard.

The following week Jimma was back at Norwich market. The parrot was on its perch.

"I know yew," it said as he approached the shop. "I know yew an orl," retorted Jimma. "Yew married a duck!"

He tried the shop door. It was locked. Jimma was sure he could see a figure lurking in the rear of the shop, but try as he might to attract its attention, no attempt was made to open the door.

After rattling the door and shouting for several minutes Jimma finally gave up when he saw a passing policeman looking disapprovingly in his direction.

From that day on, for reasons which the Gal 'Liza could never fully understand, Jimma never showed any more interest in visiting Norwich market.

11. Aunt Gertrude Not Amused

"Thass a rum ow' job gittin' so intimate wi' a cow nearmed after somebodda's greart Arnty," thought Ow Jimma on the occasions when he milked Gertrude. "By orl accounts, that ow gal never give out much o' the milk o' human kindness."

Apart from being allowed to groom Gypsy occasionally, Jimma's work for Farmer Greengrass gave him very little regular contact with the farm livestock.

He reaped and sowed and ploughed and mowed, and was a Farmer's Boy, as the old song puts it.

True, there was always stone picking, the worst job on the farm. But, if he were honest, he would tell you that, although there was very little choice of employment for young people in the country in those days, he quite enjoyed his work.

It was straightforward honest toil and it kept Jimma close to nature and all the things he loved.

He knew the birds and animals by their country names and could pause in his work to spot the bright flash of colour that betrayed the presence of that spectacular but shy bird, the jay, in a hedgerow.

Working anywhere near the river he could observe the contrasting techniques of those consummate fish catchers, the heron and the kingfisher, and he could appreciate the graceful flight of the "ow harnser" (heron) as it glided in over the reed beds.

He had seen a rabbit efficiently mesmerised by a stoat and then even more efficiently killed by a lethal nip behind the ear.

Marsh harriers? Yes, he knew them when he saw them - and kestrels and badgers and foxes and pheasants and partridges and magpies.

The countryside was a noisy and populous place and Young Jimma, in whom a poetic streak lay deeply hidden, felt a part of it. An observer privileged to be let in on the secret lives of the birds and animals he met every day.

If the air was heavy of an evening and the billy witches (thunder flies) were about in large numbers, then he knew bad weather was on the way.

Bishey barny bees (ladybirds) were welcome in his garden. And what was that tapping sound just outside the back door as dusk was creeping up? Only a mavish (thrush) troshin' a dodman (snail) on a stone to break its shell.

Nature was like that. One species providing food for another. But it was all kept in balance; all part of the great scheme of things.

And if, in springtime, he could witness the miracle of resurrection all around him, the dead brown trees and hedgerows becoming green again with all the life of spring and the power of love, and romance in the balmy air, then was it really impossible for a crucified man to return to life?

Greater miracles were happening all around him all the time.

Jimma's was a simple philosophy. Because everything in nature had a reason for existing, a season to flourish and a season to die, it must all be part of some great plan. It hadn't just happened like that.

Although he would not have put these thoughts into words, Jimma loved it all; every little jenny wren and robin and skylark and curlew.

As one East Anglian farmer once famously put it: "If Heaven was better than this I'd go today. But I doubt if it is, so I'll try and hang around a bit longer!"

But even Paradise has its drawbacks. The villains of Jimma's life were the pigeons and rabbits which invaded his garden, the foxes which attacked his chickens, and the rooks and crows which feasted on the newly seeded fields, blissfully ignoring the turnip headed scarecrow whose outstretched raggedy arms, flapping in the wind, failed to make any impression on them at all.

But even pigeons and foxes and rooks and crows were part of nature. Eating people's crops and chickens was what they did, and Man was their natural predator. His purpose in the great plan was to help preserve the balance of nature by controlling the numbers of those species which made his life difficult.

What harm, then, if he and his friends did enjoy the bonus of crusty home cooked pies filled with the rabbits or pigeons they had shot. It was called living off the land.

Married he might be, but Jimma's workaday life had hardly changed at all since the days when he had been tied to his mother's apron strings. Only now the chores he had to do each evening after tea were his own and not his father's. Sam and Bram, the two friendly labradors that walked to his heel, were his own. So were Bertha the sow, and Gertrude the cow, and they all needed his care and attention which he gave most willingly.

The Gal 'Liza would have fed the chickens, collected the eggs and milked the cow during a busy working day filled with cooking, washing, cleaning, making butter, jam and preserves in due season, pickling onions - and, just maybe, having time for a chat with friends at the village shop or down at the Women's Institute.

Of all the animals, Bertha the sow was to have the biggest impact on Jimma's family life. "There's suffin up wi' the ow gal," he told his father one day. "She hent bin harself leartely."

"Normally she's a contented ow thing, but jist this last few days she're bin behearvin' suffin queer. She keep a rollin' around in the muck and gittin' harself inter a hell of a mess."

"Who are yew a-torkin' about, the gal 'Liza?" asked Father, puzzled and seeking clarification.

"Blast no!" said Jimma. "Ow Bertha, my ow sow. Jist 'cos 'Liza dived inter a muck heap once thet don't mean she mearke a habit o' rollin' around in the muck."

"Blast I'm relieved ter hear that," said Father. He had encountered this phenomenon before in sows but never in wives. "There ent nothin wrong wi' Bertha," he said. "That only mean she's reddy ter hev a litter o' piglets.

"What yew wanta dew is tearke har round ter ow Wally Hogg. He're got an ow boar what shud see har roight. Mind yew, that'll cost yer 'cos I think he charge about five bob (shillings) a time."

Jimma, remembering the rabbits he had kept as a child, still had a less than detailed knowledge of the mechanics by which young were produced. He knew that it needed a male and a female, and he understood the vague outline of the process. He also recognised that he and the Gal 'Liza would have to do something similar if they decided they wanted a family.

But what he didn't realise was that sex was a pleasurable pastime as well as a functional activity. "How am I a-gorn ter know when that ha' struck an' there'll be piglets on the way?" he asked.

"Well orl yew're gotta dew is keep a sharp eye on the ow sow," said Father. "Yew c'n see har sty from yar bedrume winder so jist yew look out every mornin'. If she's up an' eatin' grass that mean she's pregnant, but if she's still a rollin' around in the muck that mean she want another visit ter ow Wally's boar."

Next morning Jimma, with 'Liza's help, coaxed Bertha into the wheelbarrow and trundled her off to Wally Hogg's establishment where the sow stayed all day and was barrowed home that night.

The following morning Jimma was looking out of his bedroom window. "Wass gorn on out there?"asked 'Liza from the bed. "Nothin' much," replied Jimma. "Ow Bertha's still rollin around in the muck. I'd better tearke har orf ter Wally agin."

Rummaging around in a drawer he found another five shillings, loaded Bertha into the wheelbarrow, and she spent another day in company with the boar. The same routine was followed for several days, and each morning Jimma, from his vantage point at the bedroom window, reported that Bertha was still wallowing in the mud.

"That musta took by now," he thought. "Thass gittin expensive a-wheelin' har round ter Wally's. But I'll try agin."

And he did; and the following morning 'Liza asked again: "Wass a-gorn on in the pigsty?"

"Nothin' much," reported Jimma, "exceptin' Bertha's a-sittin' in the wheelbarrer an' she're got a bluddy greart smile on har fearce!

"I'll hatta gorn hev a ward wi' ow Wally ter find out what that boar dew ter mearke har feel so happy. Or maybe I'll hatta tearke a day orf wark an' stay an' watch."

Now Bertha was a sow of unusual intelligence. She had also reasoned that she must be pregnant by now but had concluded that there was no harm in making sure.

Living alone, she was also a sow who liked her privacy so she took a dim view of performing in public - or, at least, while being watched by Jimma and Wally in deep and intimate conversation.

Wally, his eight children bearing testimony to his own prolific talents, was full of good advice. And in the sty the boar was masterful in overcoming Bertha's uncharacteristic coyness.

That night Jimma's mind was filled with new and exciting ideas. "How about yew not botherin' ter put yar curlers in ternight 'Liza, and me leavin my pyjamas orf an' us tryin' ter hev a bit o' fun?" he said as they sat round the tea table.

"If that suited Bertha, you never know but that might suit us as well! My Ma allus towd me that wus part o' nearture."

Liza looked surprised. "Blast if the penny hent dropped at last," she muttered to herself. And then, to Jimma: "Well, I'm reddy. Dew yew think yew're man enough fer it?"

"Well, there's no time like the present," said Jimma decisively, and they hurried upstairs and undressed.

"Oooh 'Liza," said Jimma once they were in bed. "Oooh Jimma," responded 'Liza. And from that moment things began to get interesting.

Meanwhile, next door, Ow Hinry was in a quandary. That was a really nice picture that the gal Dierdre had painted of him, but was his bedroom the right place to hang it?

After all, the gal did come and call on him occasionally and that wasn't right and proper for him to show her up to his bedroom to prove that the painting was still on his wall.

Perhaps it would look better hanging over the fireplace in his kitchen and then she could see it as soon as she came in.

Yes, Ow Hinry decided, the kitchen was the place for the painting. So he took it down, and taking the claw hammer from his shed again, he yanked the six-inch nail out of the wall.

Events had reached a climactic moment in the creaking bed next door. Jimma, his heart singing with joy, was dominantly on top and in thunderous action when the heavy frame of Great Aunt Gertrude's picture hit him plumb on the back of the head. He went out like a light.

The Gal 'Liza extricated herself, with difficulty, from underneath Jimma's inert form and stood looking at the bed with horror. All she could see was the stern and disapproving face of Great Aunt Gertrude staring back at her accusingly.

"I'm s-sorry Aunt g-Gertrude," she stuttered apologetically. "I know yew wudn't have approved o' what Jimma an' me jist got up tew."

Then, taking her courage in both hands, she added: "But yew'll jist hev ter like it or lump it, 'cos thatta took Jimma a duzzy long time ter git round tew it, an' I aren't a-gorn ter put 'im orf now!"

Great Aunt Gertrude seemed to answer with a sigh and a muffled "Ooooooooh 'Liza!" At which point 'Liza suddenly realised that Jimma was in danger of suffocating under the weight of the portrait.

Quickly she removed the stern old lady from the bed. Jimma rolled over, a serene and blissful smile spreading across his face.

"Ooooooh 'Liza," he repeated. "Ow Wally did say sex wus suffin' wunderful but I din't reckon on it bein' like that! That wus a knock-out!"

He scrambled out of bed, rubbing the back of his head. "I'll stick yew a plarster on that lump," said 'Liza considerately.

Together, their arms around each other, they looked out of the window. Bertha was up on her feet and contentedly eating grass. And was that a knowing smile on her face?

In due time the sow produced nine healthy piglets and 'Liza gave birth to a bonny baby boy.

"I'm called Jimma, so wus my dad an' his dad afore him," said Jimma, looking proudly at his wife as she held the red and wrinkled infant to her breast. "Let's call 'im Fred."

Nobody bothered to consult Great Aunt Gertrude. She was banished to the shed where her portrait lay forgotten for many years under a pile of garden tools, bits of wood and old furniture.

"Well anyway," remarked 'Liza. "The sorft ow gal never knew what she wuz missin'."

12. A Bad Day to Start a War

Ow Jimma demonstrates the ancient rural art of telling the time with the aid of a cow's backside

Young Fred may not have shared his father's name but he did inherit his infant tendency towards sickliness. The Gal 'Liza was for ever taking her son to the large house in which the doctor from the nearby town held his surgery twice a week.

"Fred wus a-blarrin' orl noight again," Jimma would say disapprovingly. "I reckon thass either teeth or he're got the gut earche an' he carnt tell nobodda.

"I reckon hevin' bearbies is a over-rearted parstime. They hully kick up a duller."

One day, after a particularly disturbed night, the Gal 'Liza carried young Fred into the doctor's waiting room to find Ow Hinry standing there.

The old man flashed a toothless grin at mother and baby. "Yew'll hatta excuse me not sittin' down," he explained politely but unnecessarily. "But I're got a push (boil) on my ars. . . . ."

"I'm suffin' sorry to hare that," interrupted 'Liza hurriedly.

"Wass wrong wi' yar littl'un?" inquired Ow Hinry sympathetically. "He dorn't harf kick up a row durin' the night. I c'n hare 'im 'cos the walls are so thin."

"Yew dornt hatta tell me the walls are thin," retorted 'Liza, thinking of the night Young Fred had been conceived. "I think he're got the cholic."

57

At that moment, as if recognising his cue, Young Fred started to grizzle and whimper. "On the other hand," said 'Liza, "he might be hungry. Do yew mind if I feed him?" "Corse not, go yew ahid," replied Ow Hinry. But he had to admit to a moment of surprise and embarrassment when 'Liza, instead of getting a bottle out of her bag, simply undid her blouse and attached Young Fred to one ample bosom.

The room went quiet - apart from the sucking sounds of Young Fred's toothless mouth - and Ow Hinry, red of face, stood looking out of the window; or anywhere other than directly at 'Liza and the feeding infant.

It was amazing that an old man who could use words like "arse" in the presence of a lady, and had seen animals feeding their young all his life, should feel so uncomfortable when humans adopted the same procedure in public.

In fact, he was gazing so intently into space that he did not notice the door to the doctor's surgery open and the patient who had been before him leave.

"Yew're next," the Gal 'Liza told him helpfully.

Ow Hinry flashed a quick glance at her and the baby. "Thass hully kind on yer ter offer," he said, mistaking her meaning. "But I hed a cuppa tea afore I come out!"

"Blast I din't mean thet," said 'Liza, now embarrassed in her turn. "Git yew in thare an' show the doctor yar push."

As Ow Hinry disappeared into the doctor's room the Gal 'Liza smiled and reflected to herself: "I dorn't s'pose thet wudda bin tew bad really. He hen't got no more teeth nor what Young Fred hev so thet wun't a' hart a lot!'

While this sort of thing was going on Jimma continued working for Farmer Greengrass. He did not appreciate nights without sleep.

Work on the farm was hard and the hours long. Especially during the grain harvest, when the working day lasted from dawn until nightfall, or in the autumn when Jimma and the other farm workers spent their days in the fields "chopping out" sugar beet.

At harvest time the Suffolks patiently hauled the binder around the fields, the first piece of automation being the moving belt and flying arms which tied the cut corn into sheafs, using strong twine.

Following close behind came the workers collecting up the sheafs and propping them into small pointed wigwams around the field ready to be carted to the stack yard for threshing.

Since these little shacks had as many different names as there are regions of England, veteran countrymen still argue whether East Anglians referred to them as stooks, shocks, ricks or by any one of a variety of other names.

There would be but one brief break in the day's work when the wives and mothers would appear with bundles of bread and cheese, and jugs of beer or cold tea.

Children, enjoying their harvest holidays from school, would be called on to help. Motivated by the coppers which Farmer Greengrass paid out for the rabbits caught in the harvest field and sold on to the local butcher, they would chase the luckless animals which were disturbed in their hundreds.

As the binder slowly circumnavigated the field, and the square of standing barley grew ever smaller, the rabbits would dart out in all directions, pursued to every corner of the field by boys brandishing sticks.

Invariably the pursuers would return in triumph, carrying a still-warm rabbit by its hind legs and delivering it to the table by the field gate. There was always rabbit on the dinner table at harvest time.

Rats and mice were also disturbed when the straw stacks were threshed. It is alleged, by the old men who remember, that the workers tied short lengths of binder twine - known as 'lijahs - around their trouser legs to stop the "varmints" seeking refuge in those warm and ticklish places where a set of sharp teeth might wreak havoc with England's future!

Harvest was also a wonderful festival in the village church which would be filled, not only with people singing the familiar hymns of the season, but also with the best gifts of produce from field, orchard, garden and kitchen.

Harvest Festival time was second only to the village produce show as a platform for the display of the best locally produced fruit, vegetables, cakes and preserves. Villagers strove to grow bigger, better, juicier, tastier gifts than their neighbours, and in church Canon Gunn would "run on" at length about God's bountiful mercies before they were cleared away and distributed among the poor and needy of the parish.

The services were followed by a harvest supper in the village hut where the tables groaned under the weight of good wholesome home produce and there was much dancing, singing and general jollity.

We are talking here about a time which was, in many ways, the heyday of the countryside. Cows grazed peacefully, water troughs and the lush grass of fields and marshlands supplying all their needs.

Strategically dotted about their grazing marshes were small wooden huts mounted on iron wheels so that they could be towed by the horses to the fields where the best grazing was to be found.

These huts, many of them very old and not unlike the privy which stood at the bottom of Ow Jimma's garden, provided mobile dry storage space and shelter for the stockmen.

To visitors from the outside world the pastoral remoteness of East Anglia made it a land of mystery whose inhabitants must be dim because they spoke a strange language, were ruled by the seasons and answered only to countryside laws which outsiders were not privileged to understand.

East Anglians were not reluctant to encourage this air of mysticism since, by appearing dumb and uncommunicative, they could weigh up visiting "furriners" before deciding whether they should be welcomed, ignored or gently teased.

Jimma would often tell of the day his father, Ow Jimma, had enjoyed his own secret laugh at the expense of "one o' them townies."

The man had been exploring the countryside and, having wandered off the road, was crossing a field in which Ow Jimma, with Young Jimma at his side, was milking a cow. The field was on high ground and the rooftops of the village could be seen in the near distance.

Realising his countryside ramble had taken rather longer than he had expected, he approached Ow Jimma and said, none too politely: "Hey you there, can you tell me the time?"

Ow Jimma, a proud and independent man, took umbrage at the visitor's imperious tone. Slowly and deliberately he turned to young Jimma and instructed: "Boy, grab yew howd o' th'ow cow's tail and lift that up as high as yew c'n git it."

Young Jimma did as his father asked and the old man closely examined the animal's filthy rear orifice. "I reckon thass about 'arf parst four," he observed after due consideration and without the slightest hint of a smile.

The visitor was mystified, unable to decide whether Ow Jimma was completely off his head or whether the old man was simply demonstrating one of those mysterious age old skills which God had vouchsafed to countrymen alone.

On balance, he preferred to believe that Ow Jimma had simply gone senile - until he got back to the village inn, where he was staying, and found that the old man's estimate of the time had been accurate.

Meanwhile, back in the field, Young Jimma asked his father: "How'd yew dew that?"

"Well boy," the old man replied in a tone which implied he was giving his son a piece of advice which would serve him well in later life: "Th'ow cow was a-fearcing in jist the right direction towards the village. When yew lifted har tearle outa the way I could jist see the charch clock 'twin har legs!"

This simple explanation did not stop at least one "townie" from dining out for years on his discovery that a countryman could tell the time by studying a cow's mucky backside!

In the days before mechanisation transformed agriculture one of the least popular jobs on the farm was chopping out the rows of sugar beet.

An often told story well sums up the nature of this job which, because of the autumnal timing of the beet harvest, often had to be done in the most inclement weather.

The second world war had darkened the skies of world events, but had not yet made much of an impact on country life.

The newness had hardly worn off the first world war memorials which, in every village, bore frighteningly long lists of the names of good honest men who would never have thought to leave their home soil had they not been persuaded that there was a need to defend it.

Men for whom a journey to Norwich or Ipswich was a major adventure had answered that call, had endured untold horrors in a foreign land, and had stayed there under serried ranks of gravestones which bore the familiar names of many an East Anglian family.

Yet life had hardly changed in the rural fastness of Norfolk and Suffolk as the storm clouds gathered over Europe again and Jimma worked alongside his friend Bert in the sugar beet field. It certainly hadn't improved for the returning heroes of the first world war and their families. And the pace of life noticeably hadn't increased.

The rain was coming down in sheets. The field was a huge mud patch from which the two workers were extracting the beet and chopping off the tops with their "hooks".

Cold, wet, but accepting their lot with a true countryman's stoicism, they worked on. "I see in the pearper the Jarmans ha' entered some plearce called Czechoslovakia," commented Bert, keen to impress his friend with the extent of his knowledge of current affairs.

The two worked on in silence for half an hour or so. Then, when they reached the end of the row Jimma straightened up. Water flowed from the rim of his hat and down the back of his neck. "Well," he remarked in measured tones: "They hent got much of a day fer it."

And no more they hed, as your average East Anglian would have agreed. They were glad Hitler had chosen to invade Czechoslovakia rather than East Anglia, but only because they felt a sporting concern for the Fuehrer's own welfare.

The truth is that Hitler, had he chosen to visit East Anglia, would have been received with much the same sort of hesitant suspicion and native reserve as that which greeted any other "furriner". Patriotic to a man, and woman, they would have first ignored him and then given him "what for", had they thought he deserved it.

Twenty years after that conversation in the beet field another Norfolk farmer was asked by a television interviewer whether he was afraid of foreign competition with Britain entering the Common Market. "No," he replied simply. "I'm a Norfolkman; they shud be afreard o' me!"

Mind you, if he had enjoyed the gift of foresight, and had known what a mess the politicians were to make of it all, he might have answered differently.

East Anglians, who after all regarded people from the next village as not being "local", viewed anybody from outside the two counties as a "furriner" and therefore to be treated with great care.

It was not that country people were unfriendly or unwelcoming. They were simply suspicious that a "furriner" might be some know-all wanting to tell them how to lead their lives. Visitors had to be "wintered and summered" before being accepted. If, having served their "apprenticeship", they proved acceptable then they were friends for life. If not, then they were to be ignored for life.

"Speak as yer find, an' dunt tearke nobodda else's ward fer it," had always been the instruction by which Jimma's father urged his son to form his own opinions about other people, "local" or otherwise.

The philosophy was well illustrated the day after Jimma and Bert had their conversation in the sugar beet field with Britain on the threshold of the second world war.

As the two worked their way quietly along the row a large expensive looking car drew up at the field gate. This was a most unusual occurrence and Jimma knew immediately that the newcomer was not Canon Gunn. The posh car's arrival had been far too sedate and steady.

The driver, a stranger to both the farm workers, wound his window down and called: "Hey, Jimmy!"

People in cars were to be treated with grave suspicion, especially if they seemed to know a fellow's name and he didn't know theirs. Nevertheless, Jimma straightened up and walked, with measured tread, towards the car.

"Can you tell me the way to Ipswich?" called the driver in a voice that Jimma immediately identified as "high falutin".

"I might be earble tew," he responded, not giving anything away. "But fust I want ter know how yew knew my nearme wus Jimma."

"Well, I suppose I just guessed," said the driver. "In that cearse, yew c'n guess yar way ter Ipswich," responded Jimma, turning to go back to his work.

Quickly the driver got out of his car. "I'm sorry to have offended you," he called, anxious to make amends for a greeting to which this man had evidently taken offence. "But I would be most obliged if you could give me directions."

Jimma relented, stopped, scratched his head and considered for a moment. "Well," he began thoughtfully: "Fer a start I wudn't start from here if I wus yew!"

"But I don't have much choice," said the driver, "considering that I'm here, anyway."

"Orl roight, orl roight," said Jimma. "No need ter git inter a mucksweat. I'll tell yer. Yew drive down ter the fork in the rud, tearke the right tarnin an' go down the hill, bear left round ow Wally Hogg's cottage - yew'll know which one I mean 'cos the gal Sarah'll hev har washin' out, seein' as thass a Tewsda (everyone else dew thars on a Monda but she like ter be dickey opposite) - then yew go down the village street, up acrorst the common and past the windmill an' yew'll find yarself on the Ipswich tarnpike."

"Thankyou," said the driver, getting back into his car and preparing to drive off. "Mind yew," called Jimma as the car began to move. "Dew yew tearke the left hand tarnin at the fork that'd probly be half a mile shorter!"

By this time the driver was losing his patience. "Trust me to ask directions from a fool," he said as the car moved away.

"I may be a fewl," shouted Jimma after the departing vehicle: "But at least I i'nt lorst!"

He never did find out whether the man took the direct route to the Ipswich "tarnpike", or went by the scenic one.

13. Active Service

Norfolkmen in uniform. Proud heroes like these kept the home fires burning, and sometimes put them out, when security was threatened during the war.

It could be said that the second world war opened up East Anglia to "furriners" more than any other period of history.

And most of the region's visitors wore uniforms, talked big, chewed gum and drove big cars along country roads with even greater recklessness than Canon Gunn had ever displayed. With the result that Jimma and his friends were never to forget the Yanks as long as they lived.

More immediately, the ageing Canon Gunn decided the time had come to sell his car and buy a bicycle.

It had taken some time for the war to make an impact on life in Jimma's village. Being in a reserved occupation as a producer of food, he escaped an early call to arms. Instead, he joined the Local Defence Volunteers, who later became the Home Guard, meeting once a week at the village hall for drill night and taking part in exercises at the weekends.

In the early years weapons were few and far between, the platoon's meagre arsenal consisting of a few 12-bore shotguns, a couple of .22 rifles and a first world war officer's pistol which had belonged to Lord Wymond-Hayme, who inevitably became commanding officer.

"How d'yer think yer a-gorn ter stop them Jerries wi that lot?" the gal 'Liza asked Jimma one night after drill. "People say they're got a lot more stuff than yew lot hev."

Jimma's face took on a conspiratorial look. "Yew din't orta arst questions," he said. "I arn't at liberty ter gi' yer orl the informearshun on account of thass a secret, so His Lordship say.

"We dunt want details o' our defensive arrearngements a gittin inter the lugs o' the enemy," explained Jimma. "They're got spies everywhere, so he reckon."

"But I aren't a enemy!" protested 'Liza. "Surely yew c'n tell me suffin. I aren't a-gorn to go blartin thet out to no Jarman spies."

"Well, I'll jist say this," replied Jimma mysteriously. "That orl depend on us hidin' in the woods and dewing suffin called gorilla warfare."

"Blast thass a rummun," remarked his wife, none the wiser. She said no more but she was puzzled. Somebody had told her that all kinds of monkeys, including gorillas, lived on bananas and you couldn't get a banana for love nor money during the war.

Anyway, she never knew gorillas could shoot. And, while she was on the subject, how come Jimma always took his darts to drill nights? Surely he wasn't going to throw them at the advancing Jerries?

She gave up. The Official Secrets Act was obviously a particularly impenetrable piece of legislation in wartime.

For Lord Wymond-Hayme the second world war came as no surprise. In his view it had only been a matter of time before those "demmed Huns" started getting above themselves again.

War simply enabled him to march around in uniform ordering people about instead of doing exactly the same thing whilst wearing plus fours, tweed jacket and deerstalker hat.

"Left roight, left roight, we hed a good hoom an' we left, roight, left, roight," sang the platoon as it marched around the village.

Home Guard service also involved doing all-night guard duty. The platoon had commandeered a boat and two-man patrols would float silently down the river during the hours of darkness, their shotguns pointed heavenwards and their ears straining for the sound of aircraft engines or the furtive rustle of parachustists creeping through the undergrowth.

One moonless night Jimma and Bert were manning the boat and had taken a goodly supply of beer to keep their spirits up and fortify themselves against the cold night air.

By the time they approached the bridge which carried the railway across the river they were as vigilant as ever, even though their faculties had become slightly blurred by regular doses of "fortification" and they were having difficulty resisting the temptation to sing a merry song.

Suddenly a voice called from the darkness: "Halt, who goes there? Approach and be identified." Jimma knew that regular soldiers guarded railway installations, the responsibility being considered too onerous for the men of the Home Guard in his village at that early stage of the war.

But you couldn't be too careful. The voice might belong to a spy who had parachuted in and was only pretending to be a British soldier. "Them Jerries" were trained to speak better English than Jimma did, especially when he had had one or two.

Emboldened by the beer, and slurring his words even more than usual, Jimma called back: "I'll tell yer who I am if yew tell me who yew are!"

"I don't have time to argue," said the voice, and a shot promptly rang out across the water. There was a crack of splintering wood and the boat immediately began to sink. "Blast if we ent in action!" exclaimed Jimma, grabbing his 12-bore, standing up unsteadily in the sinking boat and loosing off a shot in the general direction from whence the voice had come.

He had no time to get in a second shot as he and Bert floundered in the water, trying desperately to keep their weapons dry.

As they scrambled towards the bank a group of shadowy figures gathered round. "HANDS UP," said one of them very deliberately. And then, even more loudly and slowly: "D-O Y-O-U S-P-E-A-K E-N-G-L-I-S-H?"

"O' corse I dew, yer grit slummeken tule!" shouted Jimma in a very blurred East Anglian accent. "Whatta yew gotta tile loose or suffin? Yew're the enemy. Yew'd better hull yar gun down an' sling yar 'ook roight sharpish dew I'll hatta tearke yew inter custady, or suffin."

"Disarm them and take them to the captain," ordered the corporal who had challenged Jimma. The shadowy figures took Bert and Jimma by the arms, and struggle as they might, they were frog marched away.

"I'll tell my gaffer about this hare outrearge!" shouted Jimma over his shoulder. "He'll mearke sure yew git yar cum uppance. Yew desarve a bluddy good larrupin, yew Jarmans dew."

The corporal, a Londoner, sighed. "I couldn't understand a word that fella said," he muttered to himself. "You'd think them square 'eds would teach their spies to speak better English."

The story of how Jimma and Bert were delivered to the local police house and had to be reclaimed and vouched for by Lord Wymond-Hayme the next day is a long one and best left untold here. Suffice it to say that neither ever achieved promotion in the Home Guard beyond the rank of private. Indeed, Jimma was later to blot his military copybook in an even more spectacular manner which almost caused him to be discharged ignominiously from the Home Guard.

The arrival of the Americans was an enormous culture shock to the likes of Jimma. He had no time to "winter and summer" these larger-than-life allies, and little opportunity to make up his own mind whether or not he wanted them to stay.

The Allies had concluded that, from both a geographical and strategic standpoint, the gently rolling countryside of East Anglia made a good launch pad for bombing raids over Europe.

Air bases were set up at amazing speed, B17s and B24s arrived in vast numbers, and Jimma learned a new word - GI. Or was it "Guy"? He couldn't be quite sure; and anyway he didn't know what it meant.

Whatever they were, GIs or Guys, these fancy blokes filled up the bar of the Pig and Whistle, smoked big cigars and talked incessantly of how everything was much bigger and better in some place called The States.

Big talkers and even bigger spenders, they seemed to have an inexhaustible supply of chewing gum with which to win over the local children, and Nylons to bestow on their elder sisters.

The latter were dazzled by these glamorous figures - every one a hero, in his own eyes anyway. Their uniforms were more stylish than the saggy battledress in which British soldiers came home on leave. And infinitely more fashionable than the hairy and ill fitting ensembles sported by the Home Guard.

In short, this "occupying army", which made off with all the best looking girls in the neighbourhood, created exactly the wrong impression with the naturally reserved Jimma and his friends whose lives and diets were now controlled by a ration book.

It was only later in life, and with the benefit of hindsight, that Jimma could remember the good times, the kindnesses and the friendships which grew up between the East Anglian population and these young men who were plunged unwittingly into their midst and asked to fight in the hostile skies of a strange dark continent thousands of miles from home.

Of course they were spoilt by their superiors. Of course they had food when others did not. But they shared their good fortune, often inviting local children to Thanksgiving parties and other celebrations on "the camp".

It was easy to forget that many of these men were dying for the hard won freedoms which would one day secure a new peace.

In their turn, many East Anglian families welcomed the Americans into their homes, especially at Christmas time when one of the farmyard fowls would be sacrificed to supplement the otherwise meagre festive fare.

By the time the Americans arrived Britain's desperate need of every fighting man meant that the regular soldiers had all left the neighbourhood and the Home Guard was left to - well, guard everything that needed guarding.

Jimma was on patrol one afternoon at the local gasworks when a large American staff car approached with an important general in the back seat. He was on his way to take command of the local air base. Jimma stepped boldly into the road brandishing the new .303 rifle with which he had recently been issued and of which he was inordinately proud. "Halt!" he yelled at the top of his voice. "Hew go thare!"

"Ignore the yokel," said the general to his driver. "Drive on, I'm in a hurry."

Jimma leapt out of the way of the passing car. But as it sped on a bullet zipped through its rear window, narrowly missing the general and whipping the driver's hat off before smashing the windscreen.

The car screeched to a halt. "Hell, man!" exploded the General. "Are the Goddam natives trying to kill us now?"

The sound of Jimma's heavy boots could be heard pounding up behind. Then his face, red and sweating, appeared at the driver's window.

"Blast if I know," he blurted out breathlessly. "Thass a duzzy good job yew stopped when yew did 'cos next time I shun't hev aimed above yar hids!"

"Aimed?" screamed the general. "You mean to say you actually aimed that thing?"

"That I did, Master," responded Jimma, adding, by way of explanation: "But yew're gotta remember I wus a-trying ter keep up wi' yer at the time an' yew wus a-gorn a bit fast."

"You've not heard the last of this," threatened the angry general. But he did make a mental note to instruct his driver that it would be advisable to stop in future when challenged by the Home Guard.

Therefore, while he certainly intended to report the incident to his assailant's superiors, he also felt that, on balance, it was probably best not to make a big issue of his instruction to "ignore the yokel."

As for Jimma; he got a surprisingly mild telling off from Lord Wymond-Hayme. "Strictly speaking," said His Lordship: "I should put you on a charge for insubordination and endangering the life of a senior officer, and you should be discharged with ignominy. But I'll let you off this time. However, don't do it again.

"Strangely enough, the Americans have made no demand that you should pay for the damage done to their staff car. But you have, of course, destroyed any remote chance you may have had of promotion in His Majesty's Home Guard."

"Thankyer fer bein' so unnerstandin', sir, and not dischargin' me wi' ignorance," said Jimma, saluting as smartly as he was able.

Jimma could be positively obsequious if he felt it suited his purpose, but he still had to stifle the sneaky little thought that His Lordship so much enjoyed being superior that he would have liked the war to go on for ever.

Meanwhile, the old aristocrat was quietly thinking to himself: "True, a senior officer was put at risk, but he was also an American and not 'One of Us', so even if the soldier had hit him the crime would not have been quite so serious. An honest mistake in wartime, perhaps."

But he did not share the thought with Jimma.

14. Black Shuck and the Ghostly Monk

Jimma demonstrates how to use the privy in safety and free from the danger of an air raid. The answer - don't install a chain!

East Anglians possess the ability to laugh at themselves. In fact, their introspection is well illustrated by their sense of humour. It rarely depends on poking fun at other people - except, perhaps, "townies" and Americans.

This is probably why very few East Anglian comedians are ever seen on television.

To be frank, the TV companies never seem able even to pitch an East Anglian accent accurately, especially in those drama productions supposedly set in the region.

During the early years of the friendly American wartime "occupation", however, there was such a clash of contrasting cultures that the Yanks had to come in for a certain amount of "stick".

Big, brash, noisy and ingenuous, it could be said they left themselves open to it.

Jimma had heard one unlikely story about a newly arrived GI who went to Norwich for a night out.

Visiting a pub, he told the landlord: "Gee Bud, I've heard a lot about that Guinness you guys drink; how it makes you strong enough to bend iron girders. Think I could try it?"

"If you think you can handle it," replied the landlord, pouring a pint.

Minutes later the American felt the need to visit the toilet which, as in most pubs in those days, was in the back yard.

While he was thus occupied there was an air raid and the pub received a direct hit, fortunately without loss of life.

As the rescue workers dug at the enormous heap of wreckage the landlord was a worried man. "There's a Yank in there somewhere," he said. "He was in the bog and thass round the back."

With the benefit of his directions the rescue workers finally dug down far enough to reach the American whose grimy face wore an expression of deep admiration and gratitude. Spotting the landlord immediately, he said with a touch of awe: "Gee whizz Mac, that Guinness don't half make a man strong. All I did was pull the chain and the whole dang place came down on top of me!"

Jimma's friend Huby was a porter at the village railway station where, in addition to the passage of about 12 trains a day (six in each direction), the occasional troop trains arrived bringing more men bound for "the camp".

Under normal circumstances Huby was a man of few words and unsmiling countenance. But the arrival of the Americans dragged him out of his shell, causing such a transformation that for the rest of his life he was seen in the village as a man of lively and inventive wit. The dramatic change in Huby was as a humble caterpillar turns into a lustrous butterfly.

Part of Huby's job was to go on board the troop trains with the military policemen and make sure all the new arrivals were rounded up and the train was empty before it was sent off again.

His would therefore be the first "native" face seen by the new arrivals. It would later be readily recognised in the tap room of the Pig and Whistle where the normally lugubrious Huby was in the habit of sipping half a pint of mild beer on a Saturday night.

He would speak to only a privileged few, and then only in monosyllabic grunts, before shuffling off home with the comment: "Well, I'd better git orf now an' show my missus a good husband."

His friends, noting that he always left before buying anybody a drink, would bid him farewell sympathetically in the knowledge that his wife had a formidable temper, was built like a Churchill tank and could pack almost as hefty a punch.

With the arrival of the Yanks, however, Huby became a star almost overnight, revealing two hithertoo hidden talents; a huge capacity for drinking beer and an ability to spin yarns about the folklore and history of the village.

But it took the Americans to drag these talents out of him. They would arrive for an evening of mixing with the natives, and as soon as they spotted Huby with his half pint they would gather round, offering him drinks and urging him to tell them a story.

Huby would spin many a yarn about Victorian train crashes. Or about smugglers bringing contraband up the river and hiding it in the village church whose ornate roof, covered in carved angels, still bore the scars inflicted by musket balls fired at it by Cromwellian troops.

He would tell of Black Shuck, the East Anglian hell hound which had terrorised whole communities in the dark ages, and whose ghostly apparition still stalked the village on moonless nights.

On such nights the GIs would look over their shoulders with some trepidation as they headed along the country road back to camp.

Some swore they could see a pair of red fiery eyes following them, and the fear that they might belong to Black Shuck turned their frequent sorties behind the hedge - the inevitable aftermath of an evening's consumption of wartime English beer -

into eerie experiences. They could deal with the Germans, OK, but an encounter with the fearsome hound of East Anglia was another matter entirely.

Some of Huby's stories would be loosely based on local history, legend and the oddments of information which he had acquired from Mr Swishem at the village school. The rest would come straight from his own fertile imagination.

The more Huby was plied with pints by the generous GIs, the more fanciful his stories became, and it was not unknown, in those days of beer shortages, for the pub to be drunk dry during his story telling sessions.

Sidney, the landlord, had mixed feelings about these evenings. He was pleased his pub was full, devastated when he ran out of beer, intrigued when Huby invested the Pig and Whistle with the resident ghost of a wailing monk, and angry when the drinkers ignored his age-old cry of "Time gentlemen, please!" in the belief that if they stuck around long enough they might actually meet up with the apparition.

At least, this was the story he told the magistrates when he appeared before them after one all-night session had been reported to the village policeman by Huby's "missus".

It had been a mystery to the villagers how Huby managed to get away with his nightly excursions to the Pig and Whistle. Until they discovered that, while Huby was regaling the clientele of the tap room with his stories, his missus was finding other ways of entertaining the troops at home.

It all reached an inauspicious climax one wet and windy night. The weather was so bad that very few GIs had ventured down to the Pig and Whistle that night and Huby went home early.

Struggling against the wind and rain he took a short cut across a cow field, losing his front door key as he staggered along, warmed by the ale he had drunk and buffeted by the wind. By the time he got home and banged on the front door he was in a dreadful state and covered in the rich odour of farmyard muck.

"Blast yew dew look a soight," said his missus on opening the door. "What hev yew bin a-doin on?"

Huby thought it was slightly odd that his missus was wearing a nightdress under the coat she had hastily thrown on to open the door. She must have decided to go to bed early, he thought.

But all he said was: "Well, I took a short cut acrorst the cow fild on the way hoom from the pub and the wind kep' a blowin' moi hat orf. That wus dark an' I tried six on afore I got the right one!"

"Yew better go round the back," said his missus. "I carn't hev yew a-comin in the front door lookin' loike that."

Huby sensed something strangely defensive in the demeanour of his missus. He hurried round to the back door, lifted the latch and blundered in - just in time to see a large American sergeant, still buttoning his trousers, disappearing out of the front door.

From then on, by mutual agreement, both Huby and his missus would go to the pub on those evenings when it had any beer - and both would return home only after the beer ran out.

15. Of God and Mammon

Ow Jimma was a pillar of the village church where his singing in the choir had two volumes - loud and very loud. And his robes bore a striking resemblance to the familiar smock.

In the heyday of the East Anglian village there may have been as many as six main centres of social life - church, chapel, school, shop, village hut and pub.

In Jimma's village all these vital amenities were grouped around the green.

The shop, which also served as the post office, was filled with a warm and heavy aroma to which tea, coffee, cheese and bacon all contributed their distinctive scents.

The shop was a meeting place, mainly for the female half of the population, and in those days before self-service superstores, there was usually time for an exchange of gossip with the proprietor and other customers.

The village hut was the all-purpose centre of entertainment - home of Women's Institute and men's club meetings, Sunday school, village produce shows, harvest suppers, Christmas pantomimes and the like.

To the chapel each Sunday went sober suited figures, hymn books in hand, to listen to the homespun and commonsense philosophies propounded by local preachers of long and faithful service, and to sing time honoured hymns and choruses with great fervour.

But the closest possible links existed between the parish church of St Felix and the picturesque 16th century thatched building which bore the ornate sign of the Pig and Whistle.

Rumour had it that, before the Reformation when the church had been attached to a monastery, a tunnel had existed between the house of worship and the ale house.

The official version of the legend was that this tunnel had provided an escape route for monks fleeing from the wrath of King Henry VIII.

A century later, or so it was said, it had been the means by which priests had escaped from Cromwell's Roundheads.

But villagers believed that it was more likely, if men of God were to be judged by the habits of Canon Gunn, a cleric who believed in sampling all God's bountiful mercies in full measure, that the tunnel had been the route by which the old monks had replenished their supplies of good English ale.

It was even darkly hinted that the tunnel might also have been a link with various other unspecified worldly services offered to the monks through the conduit of the village ale house. Of course, there were those cynics who suggested that the colourful history of the Pig and Whistle resided mainly in the imagination of Huby, whose wartime stories had so entertained the visiting GIs.

Sidney, the landlord, had realised that now the Yanks had gone Huby's yarns could be a commercial asset to his pub. In the years after petrol rationing and before the breathalyser, the drinking population was becoming more mobile and it was possible, if you had a good enough pub, to entice visitors from neighbouring villages. But you had to have an attraction - and that was where Huby came in.

In an increasingly competitive world Sidney was ever ready to employ Huby's talents as a story teller, and to share the fruits of his imaginative researches into the history of the Pig and Whistle with any customer thirsting after local history.

After all, hadn't Huby invented the legend of the inn's ghostly monk? And didn't he enjoy titillating the imaginations of his listeners with vague suggestions that, where the old monks were concerned, the phrase "dirty habits" did not refer to their laundry?

Huby's fame spread far and wide. And by the time Ow Jimma and Young Jimma were numbered among the regulars at the Pig and Whistle the convivial links between village church and village inn had been happily reinstated.

The pub was the place upon which the older members of the church choir converged every Friday evening after choir practice and every Sunday after morning service. Singing was thirsty work and on Sundays they had to lubricate their vocal chords ready to perform again for Evensong.

While Canon Gunn was back in the Vicarage savouring the several medicinal glasses of sherry which preceded his Sunday lunch, his dedicated singers would be in the Pig and Whistle downing pints of mild and bitter, and playing games of "pookey die" (dice) to decide who should buy the next round.

Strictly speaking, "pookey die" was a game on which the law frowned and Sidney kept the damning evidence carefully hidden under the bar counter, producing it only when everyone in the tap room was known to him and there was no danger of the village constable calling in for a drink.

These Sunday dinnertime sessions, of which the choristers sincerely (but mistakenly) believed Canon Gunn to be ignorant, sometimes lasted longer than the participants had intended.

On these occasions the ritual Sunday roast would be delayed and at Evensong the performance of the choir - which, in any case, recognised only two volumes, loud and very loud - would be particularly stentorian.

The efforts of Miss Winifred Bell, as her increasingly arthritic hands struggled to find the right notes on the organ, would be drowned by the choir's raucous and off-key rendering of "Oh God our help in earges parst; Our hoop in yares ter come."

Poor Winifred was further hampered by the fact that in those days before the arrival of electricity in the village Young Jimma's job was to blow the organ.

This involved retreating into a confined and dusty space behind the instrument and pumping a worn wooden handle, the amount of air in the bellows being indicated by a small lead weight suspended on a string.

If the Sunday dinnertime session at the Pig and Whistle had been particularly convivial Jimma might have difficulty focussing on this piece of lead with the result that the organ sometimes expired with a pathetic squeak in the middle of a hymn.

Hidden away from the public gaze, Young Jimma also had difficulty staying awake during even the most thunderous of Canon Gunn's Evensong sermons.

A knowing twinkle would creep into the glazed eyes of a congregation anaesthetised by a long sermon when the Canon, having delivered his final dramatic flourish, would announce the next hymn, only to be greeted by a silence punctuated by the sound of gentle snoring from behind the organ.

Miss Bell would manoeuvre herself off the organ seat, with difficulty, smile wanly at the congregation, and disappear. The snoring would be replaced by a muffled spluttering, a slurred apology and the sound of fevered pumping before the organist reappeared and the service could continue.

It was Canon Gunn's proud boast that he could preach a sermon on any subject under God's sun. And it was after an unusually joyful session at the Pig and Whistle that Ow Jimma, who sang a lusty bass and was seated next to the Vicar for Evensong, was emboldened to put him to the test.

As the Canon prepared to make his way to the pulpit Ow Jimma slipped a grubby piece of paper into his hand. Arriving in his lofty perch the Vicar unfolded the paper and saw the one word: "constipation".

To preach a sermon on constipation, now there was a challenge! But the good Canon was equal to it.

Thinking quickly, he began: "My dear friends; my theme for today is. . . 'and Moses took two tablets and went up into a mountain'."

During the next 45 minutes Ow Jimma was to regret his rash decision to challenge the Vicar.

The Ten Commandments were Canon Gunn's favourite subject and he railed eloquently against the wickedness of those who indulged in a life of debauchery in such dens of iniquity as the tap room of the Pig and Whistle wherein they talked of nothing else but adultery and fornication.

How Canon Gunn knew all this, of course, was anybody's guess.

Ow Jimma, whose many years of patronage of the Pig and Whistle were beginning to affect the efficiency of his bladder, was further embarrassed by an urgent need to creep sheepishly out of church before the sermon had ended.

The Canon, revelling in his moral victory, pointed dramatically at Ow Jimma and declared exultantly: "And there, my friends, goes a wretch who cannot bare to face up to the truth of my message of sobriety and moral fortitude. I rest my case."

With that he announced the next hymn, returned to his seat - and surreptitiously took a swig from the hip flask which he always carried in the pocket of his cassock.

Out in the dark churchyard Ow Jimma, still wearing his choir robes, hitched them up and relieved himself behind a gravestone. Only a thin sliver of moon relieved the blackness of the night, and as the old man stepped back, readjusting his dress, disaster struck.

He had never been able to come to terms with that new invention, the trouser zip. "Thass like openin' booth barn doors ter git a wheelbarrer out," he had protested.

Doing up fly buttons was therefore a protracted operation, especially when hampered by choir robes. As he struggled awkwardly, he stepped backwards - and fell straight into an open grave.

At that moment Charlie "Dinga" Bell was walking home through the churchyard with his faithful collie dog Ben at his heel.

He had dug the grave that afternoon in preparation for a funeral the following day, and while the rest of the village was in church he had been imbibing rather too freely in the Pig and Whistle where Huby had been regaling him with stories of the ancient monks and the church tunnel.

As Dinga moved unsteadily through the churchyard a blood curdling yell rent the night air.

Frozen to the spot, both Charlie and Ben watched, terrified and whimpering (at least the dog was whimpering), as they vaguely discerned a figure, dressed in what looked like a monk's habit, rising from the earth in front of them and uttering fowl oaths which sounded decidedly medieval.

"Blast," thought Dinga, trembling. "I musta dug thet grearve a bit tew deep. I're hit that ow tunnel and distarbed the spirits o' them monks."

With that, he turned on his heel and hurried back to the Pig and Whistle, followed by Ben, his tail between his legs.

It is a pity that Ben was unable to keep his tail between his legs. But the dog was getting old and nasty shocks tended to have a bad effect on his stomach.

As they approached the door of the Pig and Whistle the dog was "caught short" and, unknown to Charlie, left his "calling card" in the doorway.

The tap room of the Pig and Whistle had probably changed little since the days of the old monks. High backed wooden settles surrounded the room and the customers placed their drinks on heavy tables with scrubbed wooden surfaces and wrought iron legs.

On one of these tables stood the shove ha'penny board, on the wall was the darts board and out the back could be found the skittle alley. The Pig and Whistle was a centre of sporting competition as well as sociable conversation.

There were no taps or pumps on the counter. The landlord drew the beer from a row of large barrels which stood on trestles against the wall behind him. Ancient beams held up the low smoke-yellowed ceiling.

Warmth came from an open fire and generations of heavy agricultural boots had worn uneven pathways across the tiled floor.

Covered in mud after scrambling out of the grave, Ow Jimma had no wish to add to his embarrassment by going back into church. In any case, with the service ending and the congregation bidding their farewells to the Vicar in the church porch, it would have been impossible to sneak back in without being noticed.

So he decided to make for the pub. Sidney would have somewhere nice and private for him to get out of his choir robes.

As his hand found the latch of the tap room door, however, his foot hit the generous deposit which Ben had left in the doorway. The door burst open, Ow Jimma crashed into the room, pirouetting on one leg and falling headlong.

He lay there, seeing stars and hearing birdsong. Sidney came round from behind the bar, drew up a chair, sat Ow Jimma down and gave him a tot of whisky. "That'll mearke yer feel better," he said soothingly.

It did - but not for long. At that moment the door crashed open again and the dignified form of the butler from the big house skated athletically into the room. If anything, his performance was even more balletic than Ow Jimma's had been. But the end result was the same; he measured his length on the floor. Ow Jimma, seated in his chair by the bar, leaned forward sympathetically. Pointing vaguely in the direction of the doorway, he said awkwardly; "Hard luck, bor; I now dun that."

The butler raised himself groggily on one elbow and, mistaking Ow Jimma's sympathy for an admission that he had been personally responsible for the doorway dollop, aimed a blow at the old man's head with his other fist.

"Yew datty ow davil," he said angrily, his normally cultured tones forsaking him in the heat of the moment. "An' yew a-wearin' that charchified get-up an orl.

"I allus thought there wus suffin funny about yar family ever since yar son come arsting fer a job an' took his trousers orf in front o' Har Leardyship.

"I mighta known yew wus a rum lot. Thare's no tellin' what any boy'll dew if he're gotta father what keep wantin' ter dress up like a parson and then dew suffin filthy like that in public."

Ow Jimma, slumped back in his chair by the force of the butler's blow, was righteously indignant. He had never been told about Young Jimma's disastrous job interview at the big house all those years ago, and it was inconceivable to him that any son of his would do anything so indelicate as taking his trousers off in front of the Quality.

"Dunt yew start spreddin' lies about my family!" he shouted, pulling himself out of the chair and squaring up to the butler.

At this point Sidney, the landlord, stepped between the protagonists, whisky bottle to the fore. Pouring generous tots for both the butler and the dishevelled chorister, he said sternly; "Howd yar duller, both on yer.

"An as fer yew, Jimma; git yew round the back an' tearke orf yar fancy dress afore Huby start tellin' everybody the ghoost o' that ow monk ha' trod in some dorg muck an' started a fight!

"I dunt want people thinkin' my pub is so datty even ghoostly monks carn't keep their feet."

Then he beckoned to "Dinga" Bell, who was standing at the far end of the bar, feeling strangely guilty - though he couldn't think why - and trying to keep out of trouble.

Thrusting a dishcloth into Dinga's reluctant hand, the landlord instructed: "Seein' as how that wus yar dorg what caused orl this hare trouble in the fust plearce yew'd better tearke this hare dwile an' clare up the mess afore somebodda else come a cropper."

Dinga, grovelling unsteadily on all fours in the doorway, was the butt of several gems of ribald wit when the rest of the church choir and some of the congregation arrived to finish off the Sabbath in a convivial atmosphere tarnished only by the foul glares with which Ow Jimma and the butler targeted each other from opposite ends of the bar.

With or without Huby's help, the story of that Sunday night at the Pig and Whistle was retold to such good effect in the neighbourhood that a glamorised version reached the ears of the local newspaper.

A few nights later a reporter, on the trail of a story which could be headlined "Ghostly Monk in Fight at Village Inn", sidled up to the bar and discreetly asked Sidney to confirm the facts.

He adamantly refused. "Thass orl a lood o' squit," he declared: "so dunt yew go printin' a lotta lies about my pub!"

Quickly guessing that he was not going to get anything out of Sidney, the reporter decided to cut his losses and stay for a drink - or two.

In the corner sat three village ancients with three empty pint glasses on the table in front of them.

The reporter, fired with the enthusiasm of youth and inspired by his editor with the thought that everybody had an interesting story to tell, approached the venerable trio.

Yis, thankyer werra kindly, they said, offering him their glasses. They would dew him the honner of hevin' a drink longa him.

They wunt in the pub larst Sunda night, and even dew they hadda bin, they wunt ha' said nothin about it seein' as how they din't want ter git nobodda inter trouble.

Mind yew, they would be quite happy to be interviewed about their life histories. They had bin around hare a long time an' yis, now he come ter mention it, they had sin a tidy few chearnges hereabouts.

"Have you lived in the village all your life?" asked the reporter innocently. "Not yit!" replied the first of the rustics. "But I wus born here an' I're bin here ever since!"

"Would you say you are the oldest inhabitant?" continued the reporter doggedly. "No," said the first ancient again; "But my friend Horry here may be. He reckon nobodda ha' lived round here longer'n 'im onless they reside in the cimitry."

"To what do you attribute your long life and condition?" said the reporter, resorting to long words. "Fags," replied the ancient. "I're smoked thatty-odd a day ever since I wus fowerteen an' that han't dun me no harm, 'ceptin' I're gotta bit of a hackin' corf."

"An' how old are you?" inquired the seeker after truth. "Ninety-fower," replied his subject.

When the reporter asked the second old man the reason for his longevity the answer he got was: "Beer; I drink seven or eight pints a night an hev dun sin' I wus a sprog. That hen't dun me no harm an' I'm ninety seven."

The third wizened and hunched figure had said nothing so far, seeming absorbed in his pint. "To what do you owe your long life and condition?" the reporter asked him.

"Wimmen!" was his emphatic reply. "I hev a diff'rent galfriend evera week an' we allus hev a high ow time tergather."

"And how old are you?" asked the reporter. "Well, if I survive till my next barthday I'll be thatty-two!"

The reporter was young, innocent and enthusiastic. He had been instructed by his editor to "bike out to that village and come back with a story - any story."

Now he was getting desperate. Nothing he had heard sounded very authentic and the last thing he wanted to do was to go back to his editor and admit defeat.

Perhaps the vicar would have something interesting to tell him. At least he might be relied upon to be truthful and not to pull his leg so outrageously as his parishioners seemed inclined to do.

He left the pub and headed hopefully for the vicarage. He did not like to be beaten, but if the parson let him down, he would just have to eat humble pie back at the office and come back to this village another day in search of a story.

Perhaps, then, he might be more successful.

16. Mighta Bin Wuss

Young Jimma advances upstairs with murderous intent. "I shot one barrel inter him an' one inter har an' killed 'em booth; Whaddaya think o' thet!"

For a local reporter to be granted an interview with Canon Gunn was an honour akin to being admitted into the presence of Royalty.

He first had to get past the formidable Mrs Gunn who quizzed him on the doorstep, requiring to know his name and business, and to see his identification, before showing him into the Vicar's study.

The fact that he had visited the Canon many times before in search of local news made no difference. Mrs Gunn was a stickler for protocol.

On this occasion the young reporter was rewarded with a "scoop". The venerable Canon Gunn announced his intention to retire at the grand old age of 83.

"I'm sure I still have much to offer these parishes," he said. "There is still great ungodliness here despite my 40 years of ministry.

"However, I feel that I should step aside and allow a younger man to bring in some new ideas. Not too young, of course, about 60 perhaps, and not too many new ideas either; the local population does not take too kindly to new ideas.

"In any case," continued the Canon, warming to his theme; "The job has not been so much fun since I gave up driving my car. There's far too much traffic on the roads nowadays to make driving enjoyable."

Considering that Canon Gunn himself had been the most life threatening hazard so far seen on the roads of Jimma's village, and that this conversation would have taken place around the late 1940s or early 50s, it is tempting to wonder what the old Canon would have thought of the state of country roads today.

In due course he retired and the parish threw an almighty party at the village hut. After a supper of all the good English cooked meats, salads and wholesome apple pies that the countryside could provide, speeches were made in praise of the Canon's long service and gifts were presented.

Afterwards, for the first time in his life, the Canon joined his congregation in the tap room at the Pig and Whistle, ignoring the disapproval of the austere Mrs Gunn who went straight home to the Vicarage.

What she said to her husband when he had been finally delivered home long after midnight, and suspended between two muscular parishioners, was never made public.

The parish had got its revenge for all those long sermons the good Canon had delivered attacking the demon drink.

Villagers had conveniently forgotten, until this moment, that he had always given the choir a "Christmas box" each festive season, knowing full well that the men's share would be spent in the tap room of the Pig and Whistle.

"Even though he're finished lookin' arter us in this parish I bet he'll still be a-preachin' in other charches till the day he die," remarked Ow Jimma to his son. "Yew'll never shut *him* up.

"But I doubt he'll ever run on about the evils o' drink agin. That'd be like the pot callin' the kettle black!"

Several eager applicants were interviewed by the "paroochial chach cowncil" for the vacancy, and some were sufficiently interested to explore the village and its church. In fact any stranger who happened to pass through was in danger of being mistaken for the new vicar.

One young man, an unlikely successor to the Canon since he was well under 60, called at the church one day and found Young Jimma helping Charlie to dig a grave.

Ben was bounding about the churchyard and Young Fred, a healthy infant by now, was busy making mud pies with the sandy earth which Jimma and Charlie were piling up. The church bells were ringing merrily.

"Lovely bells," remarked the young man conversationally. "What?" shouted Jimma, straightening up from his work.

"I said what lovely bells you have," repeated the hopeful cleric. "Sorry Master, I carnt hare yer fer them bluddy bells," screamed Jimma. "I dunt half wish …"

79

At that moment, as if the bell ringers had anticipated Jimma's fervent prayer, the din from the tower ceased abruptly. "… them buggers wud stop that bluddy row," he yelled, completing his sentence at the top of his voice.

The visitor, a sensitive young man who had led a sheltered life and was not accustomed to being shouted at, was shocked to think country people used such language - and in a churchyard, too, surrounded by all their ancestors.

But Christian forbearance overcame his sensitivities and he continued the conversation with a question. "It's a lovely church; do you have Mattins here?"

"Blast thass a rummun yew shud arst that," replied Jimma. "We used tew but we're got Linoleum down now!"

The young man decided to have another try. "I see the flag is flying from the top of the church tower," he said. "Why is this?"

"Well," explained Jimma, his voice dropping respectfully. "Thass 'cos we're got a bishop comin' ter preach on Sunday. We thort we'd stick the flag up."

"But why is it flying at half mast?" persisted the visitor.

Jimma's voice dropped to a hoarse but even more respectful whisper as he moved closer to explain: "Thass a mark o' respect 'cos he's one o' them Sufferin' Bishops."

The newcomer could hardly believe what he was hearing. How could he possibly consider ministering to such ignorant people?

Nevertheless, he turned his attention to Young Fred, still playing happily with the earth.

"And what are you doing, my little man," he inquired, squatting beside the lad.

"Playin' confirmearshuns," came the answer. "That big muck pie is the bishop an' orl them little muck pies are the people bein' confarmed."

"So why is the bishop a bigger mud pie than the others?" asked the young man, trying hard to show genuine interest.

"Well I once hard ow Canon Gunn tellin' my Grandad that that tearke an awful lotta muck ter mearke a bishop," explained Young Fred innocently. "He reckon thass why he never got ter be one!"

The young man never pursued his application for the position of Vicar in Jimma's village, and in due course the parish was linked to several others in a countryside team ministry.

"Thass a duzzy good job Vicars ha' got bikes these days," remarked Ow Jimma. "The number o' charches they hatta look arter."

Meanwhile the villagers, ever eager to defend long established traditions, continued to maintain close links between the church and the Pig and Whistle.

The choristers continued to enjoy Sidney's dubious hospitality, and he to welcome their after-church celebrations.

Sidney was your ideal village pub landlord in all respects except for three minor irritations. It was generally believed that he had "an eye for the ladies" though no serious misconduct with them had ever been proved.

He also had something of a reputation as a practical joker. And he was sadly afflicted with a serious but irritating facial twitch which resembled nothing so much as a conspiratorial wink.

Otherwise, he was a genial host who kept his cellar at just the right temperature and served a good pint "straight from the wood".

He joined in the noisy games of darts, pookey die, cribbage and phat[1] which took place in the tap room.

He also plied Huby with just enough drink to get him started on his tales of ghosts, smugglers and Black Shuck.

A battered piano stood in the corner on which any visitor who could get a tune out of it was invited to Roll Out the Barrel or Pack Up his Troubles.

The piano, which had been much used by the Americans during the war, had now seen better days, and not all the notes sounded. Those that did were tinny and out of tune. But occasional sing songs provided light relief from Huby's monologues.

So far as Young Jimma was concerned, Sidney's most irritating habit was his tendency to say "Mighta bin Wuss."

It did not matter what disaster befell any of his customers, or how eloquently they told him the story of their accidents and mishaps, Sidney could always be relied upon to respond with the lurid details of some catastrophe which had befallen him and was ten times worse.

And Sidney's revelations were always preceded by the comment: "Mighta bin wuss."

The stories Sidney told may not always have been true, given his other irritating talent as a practical joker, but you never really knew . . . . .

One night Jimma decided to meet Charlie Bell at the Pig and Whistle, but when he arrived there was no sign of the grave digger.

"Where's Dinga ternight?" inquired Jimma. "Winnie reckon he're got a dose o' the runs," replied Sidney descriptively. "He're towd har I musta sarved him a pint what wus orf."

"When wus this?" asked Jimma. "Yisty dinnertime," said Sidney. "Mind yew, he did hev ten pints so I dorn't know how he knew which one on 'em wus orf."

"Are yew sure thass wass wrong wi' him?" asked Jimma. "He cud be dead fer orl yew know."

The germ of an idea had taken root in Jimma's mind and there was a mischievous twinkle in his eye.

Here was his opportunity to take his revenge on Sidney for all those "Mighta bin wuss" occasions which he and others had endured during long and otherwise convivial nights at the pub.

Jimma resolved, on the spot, to tell Sidney the most unbelievable story he could think up; the sort of story which would finally leave the loquacious landlord speechless.

If he heard Sidney say "Mighta Bin Wuss" once more, he'd be sorely tempted to …well never mind. But violence might be on his mind.

"Know what happened ter me larst noight?" he inquired rhetorically. "I went hoom from wark, went upstairs ter chearnge an' dew yew know what?…"

Sidney assured Jimma that he did not know what. "I went inter the bedrume an' there wus my Missus in bed longa ow Dinga Bell an' neither on 'em hed a stitch on," continued Jimma.

"Know what I did?" Again Sidney shook his head. "I went downstairs agin and took my ow 12-bore off the wall where that wus hangin' up, looded har up and shot one barrel inter him and the other inter har an' killed 'em booth. Whaddya think o' thet!"

Jimma stood back to watch the effect this revelation might have on Sidney. But the landlord was surprisingly unmoved. "Mighta bin wuss," he said calmly.

Jimma exploded. "Whadda yew mean 'mighta bin wuss'. I're towd yew the best story I cud think up an' yew still say 'mighta bin wuss'. Whass up wi' yew?"

"Well," replied Sidney. "Dew yew'd ha' come home and dun that the night afore yew'd ha' shot me!"

Jimma was dumbfounded. "Whadda ya mean?" he began aggressively. "That wus orl a lood o' lies what I jist towd yew. My Missus ent loike that!"

But however hard Jimma tried to get more out of Sidney, the landlord remained uncharacteristically silent, simply winking in that irritating way of his.

Jimma couldn't believe that the Gal 'Liza had been up to any tricks like that. She wasn't that sort of a mawther. But the problem was that, where Sidney was concerned, you never could tell . . . . .

Nevertheless, Jimma decided not to have a row with 'Liza that night, confining himself simply to bestowing some old fashioned quizzical looks on her - and just wondering. The evil seed of doubt had been sown. But Jimma pushed it to the back of his mind, even though, as the weeks went by, 'Liza's persistent "queer" feeling developed into morning sickness and in due course she announced that their second child was on the way.

Jimma continued to push all those nagging doubts into the deepest recesses of his mind. He was happy, 'Liza was happy, even Young Fred was happy. The world was a wonderful place.

Liza's time arrived and she gave birth to a healthy baby girl with ruddy complexion and a good pair of lungs.

For the second time Jimma was a proud father. 'Liza looked lovingly at him as he bent over the cot to admire the new arrival.

Suddenly he straightened up, his face red with rising emotions. "Blast if I know," he exploded. "That little bugger jist winked at me!"

¹ Phat - A card game similar to partner whist and much played in East Anglian pubs in those days. It still survives in a very few.

17. There's A Bomb in My Bucket

"I know; I'll git rid o'th'ow privy an' the hand grenearde at the same time. I'll sling it in the privy." But Jimma's plan had unexpected and disastrous results.

Belatedly realising that the decision to name their first child Fred had been a devastating departure from generations of family tradition, Jimma and the Gal 'Liza decided to call their daughter Jemima.

It was the nearest female name they could think of to Jimma.

It seemed to Jimma that 'Liza was unusually anxious to please him. She was quite happy for the child to be named Jemima, but only on condition that she should also be given a second christian name, Cyd (pronounced Sid).

Jimma puzzled over this when he gave details of the birth to the registrar. But when he asked 'Liza why she had chosen the name she had a perfectly plausible explanation.

She had been to the cinema in the nearby town and had seen a film starring an actress popular at that time, Cyd Charisse. She had enjoyed her performance so much that she felt Cyd would be a lovely name for the baby.

Jimma seemed satisfied. If his mind was troubled about having a daughter called "Sid" who was afflicted by a facial twitch which became more and more evident as the child grew older, he kept his doubts to himself.

In true East Anglian fashion he thought: "If I dorn't say nothin' I wunt hear suffin I dorn't wanta know."

As the child grew up the Gal 'Liza said nothing, Jimma said nothing, Sidney retired and the Pig and Whistle briefly became an upmarket restaurant before the business failed and the village pub closed its doors for the last time to be converted into a private house.

Occasionally, when Jimma was at work, 'Liza would take Jemima round to the old people's home where Sidney now lived. The talk would all be of happy times past, but the old publican and the child would sit winking at each other as if sharing their own little secret.

Meanwhile, there were other changes in the lives of Jimma and the Gal 'Liza. Ow Hinry, their next-door neighbour, died and Farmer Greengrass agreed that Jimma's parents, now getting very old, should take over the old man's cottage.

This way they would be close to their family and could be looked after in their declining years.

There had been many changes on the land. Increased mechanisation meant that fewer men were employed on the farm and there was less demand from the workers for tied cottages.

Farmer Greengrass, who had rented his farm for years from Lord Wymond-Hayme, now owned it himself, having been able to buy it when the estate was broken up after the death of His Lordship.

Had he been a less kindly man, he might have been tempted to sell both Jimma's and Ow Hinry's adjoining cottages to some rich "furriner from Lunnon" who would have knocked the two into one luxurious home simply for use during weekends and holidays.

But he valued the friendship of the old villagers, and recognised their lifetimes of loyal hard work. Jimma's parents duly moved in next door at a very modest rent.

The move was not without its hazards, however. The two cottages had received a certain amount of modernisation.

Electricity had been installed, water now came from taps instead of the backyard pump, and new indoor toilets had rendered the old privy down the bottom of the garden redundant.

Young Jimma had not yet been able to bring himself to the decision to get rid of the privy. He reasoned that he had spent happy times in there, trying to read the little squares of newspaper hanging from their string, and he had a sentimental attachment to the place.

It sat at the bottom of the garden, increasingly decrepid and covered by a riot of rambler roses - and neglected by all but Ow Jimma.

Force of habit drove him to continue using the privy in preference to the indoor toilet. He was suspicious of all these new fangled ideas, anyway. To his mind, the old ways were the best, and things like indoor privies were only a passing fad.

In fact, to say that Jimma's parents were confused by all these changes in their way of life is an under-statement. Neither of them could get accustomed to using the new facilities.

It was a mystery to Jimma's mother how it was possible to cook the dinner, wash the clothes or dry your hair simply at the flick of a switch. And when a light bulb failed she would be thrown into total disarray, searching desperately in the shed for the old Tilly lamp.

One day Ow Jimma rushed round to his son's house in a high state of alarm. "Blast Father, yew in't harf in a mucksweat," said Young Jimma. "Wass up?"

"Thass yer mother," said the old man. "I reckon she're finally gorn orf har hid an' gotta tile loose, or suffin."

"What mearke yew say that?" inquired Jimma, worried now.

"Well she seem ter think she's a 'lectric light bulb," said Father. "She's up on the tearble hangin' onta the wire an arstin' me ter switch har orf.

"Corse I carn't touch no switches wi' har up there like thet. No-one know what moight happen dew she git lit up! She's actin' sorft enough already."

Young Jimma hurried next door, closely followed by his father. True enough, Mother was standing on the large scrubbed wooden table in the kitchen holding the flex which hung from the ceiling.

"Yew carn't hev har standin' up there like that!" declared Young Jimma. "She mearke the plearce look ontidy. Git har down at once!"

"That en't ser easy as yew seem ter think," responded Father. "Dew I git har down orf-a that there tearble we'll orl be in darkness!"

Young Jimma gave his father a puzzled look. "Thass yew wass harf loight, yew silly ow fewl," he said in a rare display of filial rebellion. "Thet on't mearke a soight a diffrence anyway, 'cos that in't dark yit outside!" "Blast, now yew come ter mention it, neither that in't," said Ow Jimma. "In that cearse I reckon yew c'n searfely come down now, Mother," he added, addressing the old lady.

"Blast thass a relief," said Mother as she clambered down from the kitchen table, helped by her husband and son. "Thass wunnerful how yew young 'uns unnerstand orl these hare new fangled things," she said admiringly to Young Jimma.

"That dorn't harf mearke yer arm earche keepin' howd o' that wire ter stop the 'lectric seepin' out when yew hin't gotta bulb in."

"Oh, so thass what yew wus dewin'," said Jimma, the light beginning to dawn in his confused mind. "Yew think that when the bulb conk out and yew unhook it the 'lectric leak out, dew yer?'

"'Corse that dew," replied Mother. "When yew tearke the bulb out there en't nothin' ter keep the 'lectric in, is there? Leastways, thass what yer father say."

Father suddenly seemed anxious to change the subject. "Shall I switch the wireless on?" he asked. The "wireless" was an electrical device of which he did approve. "That must he time for Much Bindin' in the Marsh."

Nothing more was said about Mother's afternoon on the kitchen table. Partly to avoid embarrassment, and partly because a potentially cataclysmic event was soon to cause far greater repercussions in the Jimma family.

On balance Young Jimma had enjoyed his time in the Home Guard during the war. His service to King and Country had introduced a bit of variety into his life, some excitement to enliven the daily routine of work on the farm.

His wartime memories were still fresh in his mind, and he had kept an old hand grenade as a souvenir of those heady times when he had leapt into uniform to defend the realm.

Of course "the realm", so far as he was concerned, was his own village and little more. He had never really thought much of putting his life on the line for the ungrateful residents of neighbouring Seething-in-the-Marsh. They could look after themselves.

The grenade sat on a shelf in Jimma's shed. He had never bothered to take the firing pin out, and in the Gal 'Liza's oft-expressed opinion, it was a brooding presence in their midst; a constant threat to life and limb.

"Yew orta git rid o' that duzzy thing," she told her husband many times. "Yew never know when that moight go orf an' blow us all outa our beds. That in't searfe ter keep suffin loike that in yar shud."

One day Jimma had a brainwave. For some time he had been dithering about demolishing the old privy. It stood there virtually redundant, and it was rarely necessary now to raise the trapdoor at the back which gave access to the bucket because that receptable hardly ever needed emptying.

There was really no point in keeping a useless tumbledown little shack simply for sentimental reasons.

Progress was progress, after all, and the privy could finally be consigned to history now the family was able to sit in such comfort indoors that they could take a whole newspaper into the toilet rather than having to read the little squares on the string.

Anyway, the space occupied by that humble little structure down the garden would be marvellous for his rhubarb. He could get rid of the privy and the hand grenade at the same time. He would simply hurl the latter into the former.

Good ideas did not occur often to Jimma, so when they did it was vital to act on them immediately. Jimma took the hand grenade from his shed, marched resolutely down the garden path and, with some difficulty, hauled up the creaking trapdoor at the rear of the little shack.

Quickly he removed the firing pin, lobbed the bomb into the bucket and retreated to a safe vantage point nearer the house.

The explosion was deafening. It could be heard all over the village, although the locals simply attributed it to "one o' them American supercillious jets brearking the sound barrier."

The Cold War was at its height and the civilian population had been advised that, at best, they could only expect a four minute warning if the Russians mounted an atomic attack.

Reassured by the thought that, if it really had been a Russian attack they wouldn't have survived long enough to hear the bang, the villagers paused, pinched themselves, discovered they were still alive, and went about their business. Unexplained bangs which left them unharmed were nothing to do with them.

Jimma's mother was in her cottage. Actually, she had gone upstairs to empty the "guzunders" and iron the bedroom curtains.

The window was open and Mother, who still had only the vaguest understanding of these new fangled electrical devices, was just leaning out to reach the top of the curtains with the iron when the blast hit her!

A large dollop of something indescribable flew in through the open window as Mother toppled out. Fortunately, East Anglian farm cottages are squat buildings and she did not have far to fall before she landed on her back in a flower bed.

Shocked but otherwise unhurt, the tough old lady struggled to pick herself up and hold her skirt down at the same time. She spotted Jimma surveying his handywork from a safe distance.

"Blast bor!" she yelled. "What the davil ha' yew dun now? Ire fell outa the winder 'cos o' yew! I shudda kep' yew locked in yar bedrume when yew wus a kid. Yew allus did git up ter mischeef."

Jimma had to admit to being surprised at the noise of the explosion, but he was still rather proud of himself.

As the Gal 'Liza came rushing through her back doorway and hurried to help her mother-in-law to her feet, Jimma gave her an accusing glare. "Thass orl har fault," he said: "She're bin a-mobbin' on-me ter git rid o' that ow hand grenearde I hed in my shud.

"I hed a greart idea. I're slung the grenearde in th'ow privy an' got ridda 'em booth at the searme toime."

"Blast bor!" yelled Mother again. "Yew shunta dun that. Father wus in there!"

"Moi hart aloive!" exclaimed Young Jimma. "I forgot he dun't git on wi' the new bog in the house."

Then, being a quick thinker in an emergency, he added: "I s'pose we better gorn see if he's orlroight."

In single file the trio hurried back along the garden path. The scene was awful. The wreckage of the late lamented privy and its nauseous contents had been generously dispersed all over the garden. Swarms of flies were already homing in on the scene with relish.

And there in the apple tree hung a dishevelled figure wearing no trousers and dangling from the one remaining sleeve of its tattered shirt which had caught on a branch.

As the figure swung round in the breeze, the rescuers could hardly fail to notice that its blackened backside was framed by the remains of a substantial wooden privy seat.

"Father!" cried Young Jimma, the relief welling up in his voice. "Are yew orl roight?"

"Yis my boy," croaked Ow Jimma, his voice hesitant and tremulous, his eyes glazed with shock. "But thass a duzzy good job fer orl on us that I din't dew that in the house, en't it!"

"Yew hen't got no cause ter feel guilty," said the Gal 'Liza as the three helped the old man down to the ground.

"That en't yar fault if yew're gotta sorft tewl of a son what go hullin' dearngerous things about willy nilly. That wun't yar bowels causin' yew problems this toime; that wus a bomb. Young Jimma bunged it in the bucket. Blast if I know why."

Ow Jimma stopped and looked at his son. Supported by his wife on one arm and his daughter-in-law on the other, he was painfully aware that it was the strength of the stout wooden privy seat that had saved him from greater injury.

He looked a comical figure with his shirt hanging in strips on his grimy body and his scraggy legs looking decidedly wobbly as he tried to regain some dignity by standing unaided despite the debilitating effect of the seat still firmly attached to his rear end.

At that moment Ow Jimma was definitely not seeing the funny side of life. He gave Young Jimma a withering look in which aggression, accusation, despair and pity were all discernible.

"I allus did say yew hed a tile loose," he remarked icily. "I distinctly remember saying ter yar mother when yew wus a boy that in a week yew wus about up ter Wensdy night.

"What the hell are yew a-doin' on hulling bombs inter privies when people are a-sittin' orl peaceful like an' mindin' their own business? Yew're hully lucky nobodda got badly hart."

With that he turned and hobbled towards the house, the privy seat swinging from side to side with each step.

Once inside the cottage, the old man discovered that it was quite impossible to dislodge the wooden seat from his anatomy. And with it still attached it was equally impossible to sit down, have a bath or put on some trousers.

With great difficulty Jimma and Mother managed to manoeuvre him upstairs to his bedroom where they laid him face down on the bed so they could wash him while the Gal 'Liza went to fetch a doctor - or a carpenter.

Later that night a clean Ow Jimma lay in bed, propped up on one elbow and soothing his ruffled feelings with his third medicinal glass of whisky, hot water and sugar, an effective remedy for shock.

His red and smarting bottom was covered in soothing ointments but thankfully out of sight under the blankets.

"I 'spose the wust thing whatta come outa orl this," he said thoughtfully, "is that I're gotta use the indoor privy from now on. I hen't got no choice!"

18. Jimma Comes of Age

If Young Jimma was honest with himself he would have agreed that his father was never again quite the man he had been before the hand grenade had landed in the privy.

True, the old man put a brave face on things, and would sometimes even laugh about the day he had been "framed" by a privy seat.

But up to that moment he had been a man of positively rude health, and now Jimma felt a twinge of guilt every time he saw his father creaking stiffly around the house.

His joints had largely seized up, and at mealtimes he would move gingerly into his chair at the table. He still found sitting rather painful.

At first the family thought the old man was "putting it on" because he liked being pampered. Every night he would insist on Mother applying ointment and talcum powder to his afflicted nether regions before tucking him up in bed with his whisky and hot water.

Sometimes he hopefully invited the Gal 'Liza to perform this service, but she always politely declined.

Mother, who had recovered well from the bruises sustained in her fall from the bedroom window, was also beginning to slow up through increasing age.

But, unknown to Jimma and 'Liza, she had her own private reasons for being worried about Ow Jimma.

She kept these to herself, and the rest of the family studiously avoided discussing the subject of Father's health in her hearing.

One day the doctor, a regular visitor by now, took Young Jimma aside and told him: "You know your father is not a young man any more. That shock jolted his system more severely than you might have thought.

"Another one like that could kill him, so I advise you to be very careful and gentle with him. Look after him; give him anything he wants. He may not have much more time left."

The family took the doctor's advice very much to heart. Gal 'Liza took meals round to the old couple and Young Jimma called in each evening after work to do his father's chores and chat to him.

"Thass jist like ow times," Jimma said to the Gal 'Liza after he had done his chores one evening. "Here I am dewin' orl that idle ow bugger's wark agin while he sit there wi' a bluddy greart smile on his fearce.

"I bet he in't so ill as he mearke out. He're got round that doctor ter git us ter mearke a fuss on 'im.

Each morning except Sunday Young Jimma and the Gal 'Liza would pop next door just to make sure the old couple had survived the night. Like most country people Ow Jimma and Mother couldn't "lie abed of a mornin'" and had to be up early even if they had very little work to do.

On Sundays, however, the routine was much more relaxed. Young Jimma and 'Liza would go next door only to find two notices hanging on the tightly shut front and back doors of the cottage.

While the back door bore the instruction "Dew not Distarb" the front displayed the awful threat "Tresparsers will be Persecuted."

Thus banned from the premises each week, Jimma and 'Liza assumed that the old couple had a quiet "lie in" every Sunday morning.

Jimma, 'Liza, Fred and Jemima would leave the old folks in peace and set off on their short walk across the fields to answer the summons of the single bell which called the faithful to worship in the village church.

The family did not pretend to possess great musical talent, but this did not stop them from forming the bulk of the choir, the two children singing treble, 'Liza trying the alto part and Jimma thundering out a melody which roughly approximated to the bass line. What they lacked in accuracy of note or words they made up for in volume.

This hardly mattered since Winifred Bell, a very old lady by now, could only manage a vague approximation of the tune on the organ which she had been playing for more than 50 years.

Jimma now occupied his father's old seat next to the Vicar. The new incumbent, the third to have briefly taken the living since the retirement of the redoubtable Canon Gunn, was an earnest young man who shared his time among four parishes.

The young cleric once remarked to the churchwarden that the hymn singing was "almost heavenly."

"You could say that," responded the churchwarden. "It's certainly like nothing on earth!"

Young Jimma had taken Ow Jimma's place in the choir with some reluctance. He did not entirely believe his father's unshakeable assertion that he was now far too old and much too delicate to attend church himself.

"Them pews are duzzy hard when yer arse is as tender as mine is," was all the comment Ow Jimma needed to send his son guiltily away.

Early one fateful Sunday morning a train of events was set in motion which was to change the lives of the Jimma family for ever.

Dawn was just breaking when Young Jimma and the Gal 'Liza, blissfully and deeply asleep in each other's arms, were wakened by a voice calling from outside their bedroom window. It was Farmer Greengrass.

Now also an old man, he was out of breath after hurrying along the loke[1] from his farmhouse. "Jimma!" he yelled, hurling a handful of small stones up against the window pane. "Are yew awearke?"

Jimma clambered out of bed and threw up the window. "Corse I am," he shouted back. "How the hell dew yer think I cud sleep threw orl that row yew're a-kickin' up? Yew nearly brook my winder!"

Then, recognising the figure of his boss in the dim light, he immediately changed his tone. "Oh, sorry Marster, I din't know that wus yew."

"Never mind about that," said the old farmer. "That seem like somebodda ha' set loight to my barn full o' straw bales durin' the night.

"Thass hully ablearze, anyway. Dew yew hop on yar bike an' go down ter the village and ring the fire brigearde from that telephone kiosk on the green."

For the first time in his life, Farmer Greengrass was regretting his refusal to have a telephone installed at the farm. He had always reasoned that a phone would only encourage his wife's objectionable sister, who lived in London, to keep ringing up and inviting herself to stay for a holiday in the country.

She would arrive for a week and stay for a month. A dry and jaundiced spinster, her favourite pastime was criticising men, especially farmers in general and her brother-in-law in particular.

Young Jimma had never used a telephone before. "What dew I dew?" he asked. "Jist dial 999 an' tell 'em yew want the fire brigade," instructed his boss. "While yew're a-dewin' that I'll try an' git some blokes ter shift some o' that straw."

Jimma dressed like lightning, took his bike from the shed and pedalled furiously down to the village green. "Police, fire or ambulance?" inquired the clipped voice of the operator.

"The fire brigearde, I think he said," answered a flustered and panic-stricken Jimma, talking to the ear piece of the instrument.

"I can't hear you caller," said the operator. "Speak up!"

"Yew better send 'em down here right quick!" yelled Jimma, effectively clearing the operator's ear wax and almost perforating her eardrums.

"Send who? And where?" she asked. "Is there an emergency?"

"I'll say there's an emargency" bawled Jimma.

It took several minutes for Jimma to calm down and several more for the operator to confirm that this was not a hoax call, and that the fire brigade was needed urgently at Farmer Greengrass's farm.

"That one had a voice like a foghorn," remarked the operator to her colleague after Jimma had hung up and jumped back on his bike.

The unexpectedly long time Jimma had taken to call the fire brigade meant that some of the urgency had already been removed from a desperate situation.

He had been away so long that the barn had been gutted and most of the straw was now simply a smouldering pile of debris.

But the fire crew were not to know this. A keen young recruit had been given the honour of ringing the alarm bells as the fire engine sped through the village towards the farm.

Eldery inhabitants on their way to morning service suddenly acquired the agility of gazelles as they leapt out of the path of the onrushing vehicle.

Its fast clanging bells drowned the dignified, measured and rhythmic "boings" which sounded from the church tower.

"Thass a good job I'm well insured," remarked Farmer Greengrass as the fire engine raced madly up the loke, passing the adjacent homes of the Jimma family, its clanging bells still creating a din fit to wake the dead. The machine screeched to a halt beside the ruined barn, with Jimma in hot pursuit on his bike.

The officer in charge of the crew stepped down and surveyed the scene while his men ran out the hoses.

"There dorn't seem ter be much we c'n dew here, 'ceptin damp down the straw and mearke sure that dorn't fly aloight agin," he remarked. "Why din't yew call us arlier. We mighta bin earble ter ha' dun suffin then."

"We din't notice it," said Farmer Greengrass lamely, thinking that his insurance company might take a dim view of his not having a telephone on the farm. But then, they didn't have to put up with his wife's sister.

At that moment the Gal 'Liza came running up the loke from the cottages. "Jimma!" she shouted desperately above the din of the still clanging fire bells. "Thass yer farther; he're bin took queer. Hop yew on yar bike agin and gorn fetch th' amblance!"

In a flash Jimma was astride his bike and pedalling down the loke again towards the telephone kiosk on the village green.

Again he dialled 999. "Police, Fire or Ambulance," replied the operator.

"Amblance, an' mearke it quick!" bawled Jimma at the top of his voice.

"Not yew agin," she responded, her polished telephone tones lapsing into the vernacular in the stress of the moment. "Moi lugs'll never be the searme agin arter yew're finished hollerin' intew 'em."

"Howd yar duller[2] an' call th' amblance," yelled Jimma. "Searme address as afore, more or less."

"Yew're sure yew en't gorn ter come back in a little while an' arst fer the perlice?" inquired the operator. "They're the only ones yew're left out so far. They moight start ter feel neglected!"

But she was speaking to an empty phone box. Jimma had already jumped back on his bike leaving the handset hanging.

Twenty minutes later the ambulance raced past the church, upsetting poor Winifred in the middle of a hymn. It turned up the loke, its bells ringing as loudly as those of the fire engine had done.

The ambulance men struggled down the stairs from Ow Jimma's bedroom, trying desperately to keep the grey faced old man on their stretcher.

After they had loaded him and Mother into the ambulance and raced back down the loke, the bells still ringing, Gal 'Liza turned to Jimma, her face grave and worried. "I think he's gorn," she said quietly.

"I know he's gorn," said Jimma. "We better go arter 'im.'

"No, I mean I think he's really gorn an' won't be a-comin' back," enlarged 'Liza.

She was right. Later that morning a taxi brought Mother home from the hospital. "That wun't no good tearkin' 'im there," she said simply. "He're pegged out anyway!"

The family was plunged into a trough of sorrow. But in the countryside life had to go on. There was a time to sow and a time to reap, a time to live and a time to die, a time for joy and a time for sorrow. But all this would have to wait. There were arrangements to be made.

Ow Jimma had left strict instructions regarding the behaviour of his family after he had gone. "I know yew'll look arter Mother," he had said. "But I dun't want yew a-mopin' about wi' long fearces. Thass a sign o'weakness an' that en't the way we dew things round here."On the morning of the funeral, with Ow Jimma's instructions still ringing in her mind, Mother was offended by the sight of the undertaker's doleful face and sober attire as he delivered the old man's earthly remains for his "lying in state" in the parlour.

"Cheer yew up," she instructed. "Yew look as though yew're lorst a quid an' found a tanner. My ow boy wun't ha' wanted yew ter look loike a wet week on his big day.

"Arter all, yew're gotta remember this's one o' the most important days o' his loife! An' I dew want th' ow boy ter hev a good send-orf."

Throughout the morning Ow Jimma's friends came calling to pay their last respects and to remark what a wonderful, kind, hard working, considerate friend he had been to all of them, whether they had known him or not.

"Thass a rum job," said Mother. "Yew never hear how wunnerful people are until arter they're gorn."

The Vicar called. Young, sensitive and inexperienced he first said a prayer then stood gazing at the serene face of Ow Jimma and simply did not know else what to say.

Finally he remarked awkwardly: "He does look well. In fact, he looks in better health than he did when he was alive."

"Thass 'cos he're bin ter see the undertaker," replied Mother simply. "That man dew hev a marvellous effect on corpses."

"But the fact that he is smiling must be a great consolation to you," continued the young Vicar doggedly. "It at least shows that he died happy."

"That dorn't show nothin' o' the sort," responded Mother emphatically. "The fact is he parst away in 'is sleep an' he dorn't know he's gorn yit!"

Later in the day the entire village assembled for the funeral service, giving their names to the young reporter who stood at the church door with his notebook.

"Readin' 'em orl in the pearper is the only way yew c'n tell hew tarned up and hew din't, I s'pose," said Mother.

The funeral was a reunion of old friends. Farmer Greengrass was there, of course, with Mrs Greengrass and her sister.

Somebody had fetched Sidney from the old folks' home. "That mearke a chearnge ter git out," he said. "An' there's nothin better'n a fewneral ter meet orl yar ow friends an hev a good mardle at the party arterwards."

Even Young Jimma's boyhood friend Jarge turned up with his posh car and his even posher wife Lavinia.

Young Jimma said a few well chosen words which basically boiled down to a cross between a eulogy and a confession. "He wus a good ow boy," said the dutiful son.

"He may not ha' dun many people much good, but he din't dew 'em a lotta harm neither, an' I'm sorry I lobbed a bomb under 'is bum. The shock may well ha' hastened his end." He chose his words carefully because he didn't think it was right to say "arse" in church.

Dinga Bell had long since handed on his grave digging spade to a younger man, and had passed on to discover for himself what lay beyond the veil.

"That wudda bin nice if Dinga hadda bin here to dew the honners fer Ow Jimma," said Mother. "He wus a good friend an' he dug a tidy grearve."

After the service Mother went to say her thanks to the Vicar. "That wus a lovely sarvice," she said: "'specially when we sang Orl Things Bright an' Bewtiful."

For the second time that day there was a pause while the Vicar searched for something appropriate to say.

"He was a fine man, your husband," he said finally. "A pillar of the local community in fact, and a stalwart supporter of the church."

"Yew aren't wrong there, Vicar," agreed Mother.

"What do you most miss him for?" continued the nervous cleric. "Is it his companionship, his lively mind or his kindliness?"

"No Vicar," said Mother decisively. "That wun't none o' them things. Truth is I miss our sex loife mosta orl."

The Vicar was astonished. A bachelor who had always been slightly nervous in the company of women - a circumstance which had caused him to be the butt of gossip among those in the village who questioned his "sexual orientation" - he could hardly imagination that couples as old as Mother and Ow Jimma could achieve much of a sex life.

"But your husband was well into his nineties," he said. "And you, if you will excuse me for saying so, are not far behind him in age."

"Yew're right agin Vicar," said Mother. "But he'd bin a fine performer in his younger days, although I ha' gotta admit he hed slowed up a bit durin' the parst few yare, 'specially arter his unfortunate accident.

"The truth is we used ter lock orl the doors ter keep the family outa the house time we hed a little session evera Sunday mornin'.

"He used ter pearce hisself ter keep time wi' the charch bell, an' the pore ow bugger mighta bin alive terday if that duzzy fire engine hanta come parst wi orl its bells a-clangin'!

"That kinda knocked 'im orf 'is stroke an' he hadn't got over that when blast me if the duzzy amblance din't finish 'im orf, kickin' up orl that row."

The Vicar was puzzled. "But the fire brigade and ambulance men were there to help," he said.

"Well they din't help my ow man verra much," said Mother. "I reckon that ow undertearker must pay them ter gi' people hart attacks an' keep him in bisness!"

Mother never did let Young Jimma into the secret which lay behind his father's sudden departure from this mortal life. But he did notice that Mother never again indulged in a Sunday morning "lie in".

While she was having her private conversation with the Vicar her son was in the churchyard talking to his old friend Jarge.

Surveying the peaceful scene in the late afternoon sunshine, Jarge asked: "Wass yar fearvourite plearce in this hare chachyard, Jimma? Where would yew like ter lay?"

Jimma took a long look round. "Over there," he said. "I'd like ter lay onder the shearde o' that horse chesnut tree alongside Little Edie."

94

"But she in't dead yit!" protested Jarge.

"No," agreed Jimma with a knowing smile. "Nor yit in't I."

Somehow, Jarge thought to himself, there was a note of defiance in that last remark of Jimma's. A glimpse into a future which would bring as many adventures as Jimma's eventful past had contained.

Truly, he had not travelled far, but he had seen life. And there was plenty more of it to be seen before he qualified for permanent residence in that churchyard.

At that moment the Gal 'Liza sidled up beside her husband. "Yew know what?" she said. "I reckon yew aren't Young Jimma no more. Yew're Ow Jimma now!"

¹ Loke = lane

² Duller = noise.

"Well bor, I s'pose yew're Ow Jimma now."
Still together after an eventful past. But what further adventures will the
future hold for Ow Jimma and the Gal 'Liza?

Other East Anglian titles available from

NOSTALGIA Publications

THE HOBBIES STORY
Terry Davy
Over 100 years of the history of a well known fretwork and engineering company

MEMORIES OF NORFOLK CRICKET
Philip Yaxley
200 years of history of Norfolk Cricket

LARN YARSELF NORFOLK
Keith Skipper
A comprehensive guide to the Norfolk dialect

RUSTIC REVELS
Keith Skipper
Humorous country tales and cartoons

LARN YARSELF SILLY SUFFOLK
David Woodward
A comprehensive guide to the Suffolk dialect

TATTERLEGS FOR TEA
David Woodward
More Suffolk Dialect in Yarns and Verse

KID'S PRANKS AND CAPERS
Frank Reed
Nostalgic recollections of childhood

LARN YERSALF NORTHAMPTONSHIRE
Mia Butler and Colin Eaton
A comprehensive guide to the Northamptonshire dialect